SCOUNDRELS AMONG US

SCOUNDRELS AMONG US

STORIES

DARRIN DOYLE

TORTOISE BOOKS

CHICAGO, IL

FIRST EDITION, OCTOBER, 2018

©2018 Darrin Doyle

All rights reserved under International and Pan-American Copyright Convention

Published in the United States by Tortoise Books
www.tortoisebooks.com

ASIN: XXX
ISBN-10: 0-9986325-9-7
ISBN-13: 978-0-9986325-9-9

This book is a work of fiction. All characters, scenes and situations are either products of the author's imagination or are used fictitiously. Any resemblance to actual events or locales or persons, living or dead, is coincidental.

Cover artwork by Christopher Simons. Contains an image by Mikael Häggström based on the Pioneer 10 plaque. Image is in the public domain per NASA policy and Wikimedia Commons.

Tortoise Books Logo Copyright ©2018 by Tortoise Books. Original artwork by Rachele O'Hare.

For Tim and Brian, the opposite of scoundrels

Contents

Insert Name 9

Session 1 23

Water Fowl 29

Engagement 31

A Four-Letter Word for Exchange 43

Dangling Joe 47

Three Men on a Boat 57

Festivity 69

Possibilities and Considerations 73

Session 2 81

A Fine Time 87

D.T. Myse's *Cold Blood from a Scorched Cat: Sweet Whiskers in the Grip of Death* 89

Second Home 95

The Search for Boyle 107

Party Town 117

The Kids in West End 121

Blackout 123

If The Invisible Man Dies and Nobody Sees It, Does He Really Die? 137

Session 3 171

Twilford Baines, Buck Hunter Unbounded 175

Slice of Moon 187

The Source of All Feeling 209

Snow, Lightly Falling 219

Outline 227

Sanguine	235
Scoundrels Among Us	243
Reborn	257
The Lumping	271
Session 4	277

Insert Name

We spend hours adrift in the aisles, lost. But it's a happy sort of lost, knowing that here we have whatever we need, enough to last.

Sugar Smacks is our favorite cereal. When we were kids our mother and father could only afford bulk, and the unsweetened variety was our staple. However, now Sugar Smacks has been renamed Honey Smacks because it sounds healthier. We still call it Sugar Smacks. Tough to change old habits.

Growing up, when we were out in the world, the "real world" as the parlance has it, we were an oddity for sure. Nine brothers, all identical twins. Nonuplets: a word unknown to most. When had this ever happened in history? Life around the house was chaotic and vibrating and noisy, with all the attention we got. Nine boys—nine children of any sex—are loud on their own, but add to the mix the regular media coverage, donations from across the globe, offers for television shows, gawkers stopping us on the street for photos...well, our household never felt like the real world, at least not in the sense that it probably does for most.

Gathering food is like walking among tended fields, plucking what is ripe for eating—lettuce, corn, beans, and fruit. Except here there is no weather, no heartbreak, no rot on the vine. The floors are waxed and glowing; the world is well-lit even in deadest night.

We are the same age, with the same face—same nose, eyes, eyebrows, teeth. We have the same cadence and tone when we speak, the same posture when we walk. We have dimples when we smile. We are handsome and athletic with dark features. We are beautiful, or so neighbors and strangers often told us. We believed it so much that we started to hate it. We hated our beauty but not our sameness. We didn't understand our sameness, certainly. Everyone else had brothers and sisters who looked different from each other. Our peers observed us with awe and curiosity, but never with love. We frightened them. The uncanny doubling, the sense that we brothers shared a hive mind—such fears nagged at any potential friend. How could they even begin to get to know us? Befriending one of us would mean befriending nine. Therefore we had no friends. We couldn't depend upon others, with the possible exception of Mother and Father, to love us. How could anyone love a boy who had nine selves in the world?

★

Red

Green

Blue

Brown

Black

Orange

Yellow

White

Gray

We were coded in this fashion from our earliest days. Little round stickers were affixed to our foreheads so Mother and Father could distinguish us from one another. Naturally, our real names faded away, replaced by the colors. The clothes we were given corresponded to the coding, and to this day none of us wears clothing of any color besides what we were labeled. Some thought it cruel of our parents, thought it removed our individuality, our "selfhood" in favor of this pragmatic, identity-less appellation. We were nicknamed the "Rainbow Brothers." We were schooled at home by our mother.

★

One of us is employed at this store, a legitimate hire. It doesn't matter which of us it is because it's all of us. He/we use the name Neal, which isn't any of our names. Or at least none of us remembers being named Neal, although once again it's been years since we were known by our birth names. Neal is a good employee: always punctual, helpful to customers, easy to work with, knows the ins and outs of the cashier section, customer service, and stocking, knows every department of this place, knows all there is to know about deliveries to the loading docks in the back of the building. Neal knows so much, in part, because he has the strength and brainpower of nine young men at his disposal. Neal rose quickly through the ranks and is now a manager, which means he has his own key and security code, which is why we elected to officially leave the real world and move in.

The store isn't a Wal-Mart, although it's the same concept. It's a regional version, a so-called "superstore" that won't be named here. Our location is not important. Suffice to say that it contains a full selection of groceries, hardware, sporting goods, automotive parts and supplies, housewares, indoor and outdoor furniture, pharmaceuticals, toiletries, clothing for men, women, and children, shoes, pet supplies, and a greenhouse. Open 24 hours a day, seven days a week, it never closes, not even on holidays.

When Neal was hired, the manager said he looked familiar. Neal smiled and said he had one of those faces.

Pickles are our favorite, but we have to keep our appetites in check. Steak and potato salad, too. Nine young men can put away a lot of pickles, steak, and potato salad, and someone would notice. So we have a system, a meticulous rotation for farming what we eat. We know which foods are about to be moved to the discount bin. We know when foods are going to be disposed. We know which foods are going to be delivered, and when, and how much is expected to arrive. We have access to inventory lists, which are easily manipulated. We can't eat what we want at all times, but who in this world can?

The surveillance system is thorough but not infallible. Cameras go out routinely, little blips appear in time signatures, little blackouts, moments lost forever.

Of course Neal has to have a life outside, in the real world. He can't just appear magically at the store every day. He drives what they now call a "pre-owned" Toyota. He rents an apartment in town. Once in a while he is required to go to the bar and socialize with his coworkers. They label him "shy" and "quiet," personality traits picked by design. When people ask questions about his life, his past, he's good at deferring by making jokes or giving vague responses that nonetheless leave them satisfied. We live far, far away from the town where we were raised.

As children our mother and father did the best they could. They were nice people, simple people. No one in their family had gone to college; most chose careers in the automobile plants. Our father worked maintenance at an elementary school, and our mother was a bank teller. When we were born she had to quit, naturally, to stay home with us. Nothing could have prepared our parents for the madness of nonuplets. Undoubtedly they harbored mixed feelings. They'd only wanted what all married couples want: a family. Instead they'd gotten a bizarre nightmare. We used to hear our mother sobbing in her room, an awful sound, helpless and lonely. Our father worked as much as he could, sometimes seventy hours a week. The first few years, when we were too young to form memories, our parents received donations: diapers, food, clothing, and money. As time wore on and the novelty wore off, people forgot about us. Or perhaps, having already given generously, they figured their duty was done. Either way, once we reached school age our parents were on their own.

Where do nine young men bed down in a superstore? There was a great deal of discussion of this question. Some of us thought it best to select a single room where we would all cram ourselves, sleeping in a tidy row. One room would be easy to hide from prying eyes. Others thought each should find his own place in the warehouse— in a crawlspace, a box, wherever—and arrange a cozy nest of blankets and pillows. This way, if one of us was ever caught, it could easily be explained: Neal would blush and say, "I'm on the outs with my girlfriend and need a place to crash," or "I had to be at here again for another shift, and it was too much trouble to go home." It's never a bad idea to play for sympathy, or to show one's dedication to the workplace. So ultimately the latter arrangement was unanimously chosen.

The music is the most difficult part, pumping through the speakers constantly. The song selection is dismal. Mercifully, earplugs are available.

Neal is an attractive man, so it is only natural that his female coworkers want to date him. Although some of us were initially opposed to excessive fraternizing with outsiders, the needs and urges of a young man are difficult to quiet. We make sure not to form any long-lasting relationships. We have an orderly rotation, and no suspicions have been raised.

When we were high school age, our parents cautioned us not to go out with girls. Being home-schooled kept us from the trappings of most social situations, but our father went so far as to impose a ban on dating. At times our mother tried to soften his position, but he remained steadfast. The trauma of bearing so many children had made him terrified of pregnancy. Poor man: to see his own children as a plague, a scourge. We liked to play with his mind. As he sat in his recliner we would approach, one at a time, in two-minute intervals, and ask the same question: "Can I go outside and play?" Nine times he would have to say yes, although usually by the fourth or fifth he would turn red and begin yelling in a loud voice that "Everyone can go out! Everyone in the world, OK?" Or we would switch our stickers around, never failing to befuddle him. He didn't even resemble us, with his squat body and sagging jowls. We suspected he was envious of our good looks.

Now and then our coworkers or our women will look at us with confusion: "Didn't you tell me the other day that you don't like Chinese food?" Or "You didn't want me on top last time." It's inevitable that some variation, some individuation, will occur in spite of our best efforts. The nearly infinite spectra of tastes and opinions, the smallest personality quirks, the intimate moments of deviation—we realize these are ultimately what humans are composed of, and these are our Achilles heel. This is why Neal must be cautious about spending too much time with outsiders. This is why we need our world to remain inside the store.

When our father died we surrounded his hospital bed: nine tall, muscular boys three weeks from graduating high school. Our father, the victim of a serious heart attack—the doctors cited stress, poor diet, overwork—stayed alive for two days before he succumbed, the surgery not enough. Seeing our faces, so stoic, hovering over him, he must have realized it was time to go. Tears came from our mother. We tried to comfort her.

Another difficulty: we can never be on the floor at the same time, together. One at a time we are sent out for farming, or for supplies like propane for the gas stove, or to take our turn as Neal. The others must remain in the stockroom, in their designated sleeping spot or in some other unseen place. We read, we watch television, we surf the Internet, we exercise.

But surely we must miss our freedom, right? Surely we cannot live like prisoners for the rest of our lives?

We understand that all people are in prisons, some more spacious than others but all of them restrictive: the captivity of homes, neighborhoods, jobs, marriages, and habits. Even the wealthiest man, able to travel unbounded whenever he sees fit, is a prisoner inside his body, his memories.

Neal has been seeing a woman named Marcy. She was a customer at the store, and he assisted her in finding the humidifiers. They've gone on five official dates and have slept together twice at her apartment. She is attractive and intelligent with a highly developed sense of humor. When Neal holds her hand it gives him a warm feeling that he hasn't had with other women. Neal has begun to imagine what it would be like to have children with Marcy, although this possibility gives Neal a deep sensation of terror. His father's fear, seemingly, has passed into him. No more mothers for these men. A few more dates with Marcy, then the end.

Father is dead, but where is our mother? She is alive, not living, in a long-term care facility, her memory a thing of the past: a funny phrase because of course this is true. We are all a thing of the past. Every moment slips behind us, every action in past tense as soon as it occurs. We love our mother, but she has been gone for a long time.

Love is a muscle, weakening with disuse. When we moved away, escaped, found the superstore, we said goodbye to our mother and didn't tell her where we were going. Her sadness is irrelevant; life has many sadnesses. She has already begun to fade like a name in the sand.

The real world:

Grapefruit, sliced. Collared shirts in nine colors. A sitcom about a family with a talking dog. The daily news. Combs and hand soap, shaving gel. Cans of beans, baked and refried. A radio playing the baseball game, its volume as low as a whisper. The cool conditioned air and the click of Neal's new shoes on linoleum.

Session 1

Q: We're alone in here, just you and me.

A: Is that a question?

Q: Do you have difficulty distinguishing between questions and statements?

A: Here's a story: This guy gets out of prison. He's been locked away for forty-seven years. Went in as a kid fresh out of high school, and when he steps back into the world, he's a senior citizen. He stares up at the sky, at the gathering white clouds, the breeze hitting his face. It's the same air, the same sky that he stood under when he was out in the prison yard, but now it hurts him, like a dull ache deep inside his bones. The vast open spaces now feel terrifying. He takes a city bus back to his old neighborhood. Of course he knows his parents are dead, his friends have grown up and moved away, started their own families. Still, he needs to go there. This neighborhood was where he spent every year of his free life. This neighborhood was *him*. But then he steps off the bus and looks around. He's shocked. The details he used to know, those vivid snapshots of memory that carried him through day after day and night after night as he stared at those concrete prison walls—it all looks different. Bigger trees, enormous, with wide-reaching arms; remodeled and repainted homes; a tire store on the corner lot where he and his friends shot off bottle rockets. Even the road itself is now a three-lane with a turn lane in the middle. So many cars rushing by, a traffic light. A bike path—a fucking bike path on the side of the road! He doesn't even know it's a bike path because he's never heard the term before, but that's what it is. The whole scene is so foreign that he questions whether he's in the right neighborhood. He wonders if his neighborhood got up one day and just left this place behind, hiked up the highway a few hundred miles and set up shop somewhere else. But then he looks up at a street sign and sure enough: Montgomery Road. He walks farther up the sidewalk, checking the numbers. At last he reaches 841, the house he grew up in. He's nervous now, though he doesn't know why. The simple act of standing in front of the old place is making his head all sweaty and his heart jittery. At that moment, a kid rides up on a bicycle. This boy is around twelve years old, and he looks not unlike the ex-con looked when he was that age, skinny and gap-toothed and starting to need bigger shoes. *You looking for someone?* the boy says. *Yes,* the man answers. *I'm looking for so many people.* The boy seems to understand the situation on a deep level, his eyes shining with a mixture of solace and pity and regret, as if he knows, truly knows, the pain the man is feeling. *Here, mister,* the kid says. He gets off his bike. *Take this. You'll find them faster.* Then the kid walks away. The man drops to his knees and weeps. He's forgotten how to ride a bike.

Q: I don't believe you answered my question.

A: There's a common phrase in our language: *tell time*. As in, *Billy is learning to tell time*. Personally, I never learned how to do this. Instead of telling time, I ask it.

Q: And what does it answer?

A: Ask it yourself.

Q: Finish this phrase: I am most happy when I...

A: ...am most happy.

Session 1

Q: Desire: Can it be controlled?

A: If you're asking me *should* it be controlled, I will say no.

Q: That's not what I asked.

A: My answer was in my statement, if you look.

Q: How tall is too tall?

A: Five-thousand feet would be a bit much for most people.

Q: Should boxes come in different shapes?

A: You mean other than square and rectangular?

Q: Correct.

A: There are tubular boxes. I've received them on occasion.

Q: Those are generally called tubes, not boxes.

A: So maybe a box, by definition, is a squarish thing.

Q: Does that make you angry?

A: A little bit.

Q: Tell me about Kansas.

A: I lived in the town of Manhattan. Just for a year. There's a university there, and a military base nearby. College kids and army kids, they like to party pretty wild. The wind was nasty, absolutely mean. It would whip up across the prairies and slap you around until you wanted to cry. Children in Manhattan have to pedal their bikes downhill, no kidding. For a whole year I squatted, never bathing or shaving. I lived in the crawlspace of a family's house, in an area no larger than a refrigerator. At night I snuck into their kitchen and drank water from the tap. Ate their yogurt and cookies and sat on the couch reading their magazines. They had shitty magazines but I didn't care, I read them anyway, cover to cover: that gives you an idea of how messed-up I was at that point in my life. About six months in, the family started noticing the smell. The smell of me, that is, my filthy body. They thought they had skunks or corpses. I remember hearing the wife tell her husband over breakfast: "It's just not a *normal* smell, Earl." Got me thinking about what a normal smell is or isn't. I sat there with my head between my legs and cried for about a month. When I wasn't in the crawlspace or reading their uninteresting magazines I was lurking around town. Sometimes I walked backwards down the sidewalks, but nobody seemed to notice. One day I pretended to be an important dignitary from Istanbul. Went into a car wash and told the kid behind the counter that in my country they had donkey washes that looked identical to American car washes. The stupid kid believed me! Later that night I saw this same kid carousing with his friends, all of them wasted drunk. He saw me standing in the shadows and was like, "You're the donkey wash dude!" That's all I was to him, and I find that sort of tragic.

Water Fowl

This boy is not hilarious. Not endearing, no. He's taunting a duck at the edge of the pond. He's not yet school-aged, this boy, and already he craves the thrill of domination. He throws a stick. Another.

His aim is lacking, though his passion is admirable. His persistence. "Boo, duck! Boo!" he calls, aiming to hurt the duck's feelings, wanting to be a force in a world that has granted him so little control. The clouds are full and ready to cry and the color of the shit spotting the grass. Twenty feet away, on a bench, Mom tends to her phone and baby. The duck, undaunted, scarfs bread chunks.

This duck is greedy, no question. Gobbling too much too fast. Perhaps the situation is partly his fault. But no. Every creature deserves the chance to eat unmolested, especially such an indecent meal as bread atop feces. The boy is shouting now, outraged: "You should be in the water!" He flings a pebble like a missile, hoping to pierce the duck's breast. It bounces playfully on the grass. The duck has no arms. The boy has no wings. This is one reason for their tension.

The mother glances up at her son and mistakes his terror for innocent play. Most mothers make this mistake. Most mothers do not see the sons and daughters they have.

This mother will not now—nor ever—acknowledge this boy's future: his bones will stretch; his aim will improve; he will dodge sadness on most days; at night he will dream of clear blue heavens and the letter V high overhead, majestically and quietly flapping toward death.

Engagement

Ron and Emma Borman left the party at 2:30 in the morning. Emma took the keys because she had less to drink. She wasn't worried about police, but she had concerns about falling asleep at the wheel. It would be forty minutes, along unlit roads. She hadn't been up this late in years.

She drove, not looking at Ron. "Why did you keep talking about the neighbors?"

"Why did Bill keep talking about taxidermy?" Ron lit a cigarette and cracked his window. "Eighteen minutes about a squirrel he mounted when he was in college?"

Emma hated when he smoked in the car. "I thought we were going to try and forget about the neighbors tonight."

"I tried."

The sky was crowded with stars. The road cloaked by pines. Pavement scrolled beneath the headlight beams, reminding Emma of a conveyor belt. When she thought of a conveyor belt she thought of her life. She thought of their son Craig. Years ago he lay passed out in the back seat on the way home from parties like this one. At least his friends had always been good enough to call. And she or Ron would carry him, heavy and limp, up the stairs to his bedroom. Now Craig was a homeowner in Grand Rapids, working full-time at the auto parts store. He had a serious girlfriend his own age. He was stitching his life back together.

Ron pushed his cigarette out the window. He reached across the seat and patted his wife's thigh.

Emma felt a rush of something, an emotion hard to name. Her eyes filled. She scanned through the AM radio. Only one station came in, a talk show about investments. She didn't listen because that sort of news had been depressing lately. She scrolled with the Search button, the scanner stopping every two seconds on nothing but static.

The Bormans were returning from Bill and Sherry's. Sherry had thrown a surprise party for Bill's retirement. Most of the employees had turned out, a couple dozen of them, along with spouses and significant others. Ron and Emma brought a bottle of wine from their cellar and a set of golf clubs decorated with a red ribbon the size of a basketball.

The party had gotten out of hand. The living room filled with people dancing to songs like "Old Time Rock and Roll" and "Kokomo." After a while a guy from Accounting jumped onto the coffee table. The crowd cheered until the accountant's leg broke through the glass. He stripped to his boxer shorts to examine himself, and everyone did shots and made jokes about his knobby knees. Remarkably, he was unscathed. Bill's wife Sherry, though, cut her finger deeply while helping clean up. Standing in the corner with his whiskey, Bill had laughed and called his wife clumsy. Ron stood by, grinning and shaking his head. Emma helped pick broken glass out of the carpet.

When Ron and Emma arrived home, Emma shut off the engine. She yawned. Ron woke with a start. He looked around wide-eyed, as if terrified of where he had found himself.

Engagement

Emma stepped out of the car. The night was cool and pleasant. At the house next door, a heavy bass thrummed. She could feel it in her stomach, pulsing. Many voices could be heard, talking and laughing.

"Every goddamn night," Ron said. He closed the car door. He didn't slam it, which Emma considered a good sign.

Emma's heels clicked up the walkway. She drew a deep breath of the peonies and lilacs, a sweetness in the air that nearly broke her heart. The security light switched on. A swarm of mites danced around her face, and she waved them away. When she got to the front door, she noticed that Ron wasn't behind her.

She went back to the car. No Ron. She walked to the other side of the driveway, nearer to the voices and music. She called his name softly. She removed her heels and took two steps onto the neighbor's lawn. The grass was damp from the sprinkler and cooled Emma's feet. The neighbor's house was obscured by trees. Every window darkened by heavy drapes.

Ron appeared suddenly at her side. "Let's go," he said. He hooked Emma's arm and ushered her toward their house.

A voice rose behind them: "Hey. Not so fast."

Ron ignored the voice and kept walking. Emma turned to see a man. He held a bottle of beer. His shirt was unbuttoned, showing a slim hairless torso. He resembled a teenager, except his face was hard. She estimated him to be the same age, late 20s, as her son Greg. The man stopped behind the Bormans' car, leaving a distance between himself and Ron. "You pissed on our house, man."

"Excuse me?" Ron said.

"I saw you."

Emma wasn't exactly sure who lived in the house next door. People came and went all the time. They were Native American, or American Indian; she could never remember the proper term. It had been difficult for the past eight months not to develop bad feelings toward these people as a group, although she felt sure, deep-down, that she wasn't a racist. But they played loud music every night, and cars visited their house at all hours. A rusty pickup was permanently parked in the driveway. On the rare occasion that the lawn got mowed, it was done by a preteen boy who didn't acknowledge Emma and Ron as they passed on their evening walk.

Engagement

Now Ron said to the man, "You live over there?"

The man flicked the ember from his cigarette. "Please apologize."

"Are you my neighbor?"

"Apologize, and everything's cool."

"To who? You?" Ron made as if to move forward, but Emma held his arm. "He won't even say if he lives there." Ron yanked free. "You're on my property. Leave now or I'm calling the police."

Ron was 6'3", 250 pounds. The neighbor was scarcely more than a boy. Emma stepped in front of her husband. "Let's go inside," she said.

The man examined his boots as if he was reading them. "I'm waiting for an apology," he said.

Ron pushed Emma aside. The man wasn't ready when Ron hit him in the face. The beer bottle clinked on the pavement. Ron leaned over the man and punched him again and again. Each thud sounded heavier and wetter than the last. Emma dragged her husband off.

The man's face was a mass of blood. Emma sat beside him on the driveway while Ron went into the garage. The security light turned off, and the world went black until overhead a blanket of stars quietly came to life.

She heard the scuffle of shoes. It was Ron. He extended a hand: "Let's go."

When Emma didn't move, he lifted her. She felt weightless and insignificant. He carried her through the front door, the same way he used to carry Greg, and laid her on the living room couch. He didn't turn on a light.

Emma thought about a fly she'd killed yesterday, a fat slow one that left a smear on the counter. She wished she had drunk so much at the party that she was unconscious. She said, "We have to call an ambulance."

"Let me sit for a minute," Ron said.

The bass from next door churned and rolled as though nothing had happened. When Emma's eyes adjusted, she could read the hands of the antique clock on the mantel: 3:25.

Engagement

Headlights moved across the curtains. Ron stood from the sofa and peered through a small opening.

Emma asked, "Who is it?"

"More partiers, a drug dealer, who knows." Ron's tone was the same as every night when he peered out their bedroom window. He had a temper, but in thirty years Emma had never seen him hit anyone.

"I'm calling 9-1-1." Emma unzipped her purse and located her phone. She couldn't dial, her hands were shaking.

"Give it to me." Ron took the phone.

She felt sick to her stomach. She remembered the retirement party, the shattered coffee table, the accountant in his boxers slamming a vodka shot. She saw Bill's wife Sherry doubled over in pain, her finger opened to the bone, blood dripping, spotting the carpet.

Ron told the 9-1-1 operator that there was a disturbance. He said he was afraid to go outside, it sounded like a fight. "Please hurry," he added.

In the kitchen Emma heated water for tea. Ron sat at the table. His eyes were wet and red, and his hair was in disarray. She realized how rarely she had seen him with his hair uncombed.

"You should wash up," Emma said.

He noticed the blood on his hand and went into the bathroom. His expression was like he still hadn't fully awakened. She thought about the man; she heard again the clink of the bottle on the concrete, the sickening thump of Ron's fist against his face. She wanted to be outside, to be with the man, to help him, but she was afraid. He could be rising to his feet, pulling a gun from his jeans and charging their house; or worse, he could be dead, surrounded by angry friends.

She stood among the familiar sights of their kitchen: the stainless-steel oven and fridge, the granite countertops, the plaque above the stove commemorating her 25 years of teaching at Saint Michael's. She and Ron weren't yet 60, but she'd taken early retirement when their son Craig checked himself into rehab for the cocaine addiction that almost killed him.

That was one year ago. Craig now lived with a bank teller named Rita in Grand Rapids. He delivered automobile parts. He and Rita had recently bought a respectable house with a backyard for the dog. Although, to be honest, Craig hadn't done any of this on his own. Ron gave Craig the money for the 20% downpayment. And Ron was friends with the guy who hired Craig at the auto parts store. Ron could never utter the word cocaine. He always said narcotics, that his boy had problems with narcotics.

The teapot started to shutter and scream. Emma removed it from the eye and wondered why she had retired. In the heat of the moment it had seemed like the right thing to do. Craig had OD'd for the second time and was facing theft charges. Ron's job at the woodburning stove company was secure. He'd gotten promoted to Regional Accounts Manager, and the mortgage was only five years from being paid off. She'd wanted to take care of her son, help him through his trouble.

Ron came out of the bathroom. His face was pale. She stopped dunking her teabag.

"What are you going to tell them?"

"Nothing. Go put on your robe."

She didn't ask questions. She ran up to the bedroom and stepped out of her clothes.

In robe and slippers, she went back downstairs and outside. The air was chilly. The driveway was flooded by a spotlight. Two EMTs in white shirts knelt beside the man. His eyes were closed. An oxygen mask was strapped to his face.

Ron was talking to a police officer: "We heard voices," he said, "all kinds of yelling." He said they couldn't see anything from their window because the garage security light hadn't come on for some reason.

A dozen onlookers were gathered beside the driveway. A woman broke from the group despite protests from the police officers. She covered her mouth when she got close to the man on the pavement. She kept yelling "He's my brother!" as the officer moved her away, into the shadows.

Emma woke at eight a.m. Barely three hours of sleep. She couldn't help it; she was an early riser. Saturday, the weekend. Ron was snoring as usual, his expression peaceful. Emma lingered in bed until nine, when the phone rang. She got up without waking Ron and headed downstairs.

On the phone it was Craig, calling to wish his dad happy Father's Day. A day early. He and Rita

Engagement

were heading to Lake Michigan the next day and wouldn't have a chance to call.

Emma slumped heavily into a chair at the kitchen table. She told Craig that his dad was at Frank's Nursery, buying grass seed.

Craig had happy news. He and Rita were engaged. "Next summer we'll get married," he said. She could hear the smile in his voice.

Emma inhaled a few breaths, her eyes flitting helplessly as if the appropriate emotion might be hanging, invisible, in the air in front of her, if she could only locate it. But it eluded her. She realized that she wasn't crying with joy and likely wouldn't anytime soon.

A big breakfast, she thought, would be nice to surprise Ronald with. Pancakes, bacon, cubed cantaloupe. He did have a long night, after all—they both did.

Emma returned her attention to the phone at her ear. She congratulated her son and managed to say they were very, very proud.

A Four-Letter Word for Exchange

Maybe we bickered somewhere along the road today. Maybe we pissed at a roadside petrol station, saving a stolen wad of tissue to wipe the mustard from our mouths. Maybe somewhere behind me I left a sense of urgency, replacing it with this lurching swell of sea.

The shore is brown and deformed. She looks west, and her nose seems to touch the horizon. The seagulls hover like abandoned kites.

At the communal campsite kitchen:

Stacked in a corner, unclean dishes cast a shadow. Sunlight pushes the shadow toward the door. She steps over the shadow, regards me with kelp-colored eyes. I wish I were a lion so I could eat her face ethically. Steam eases out of the pot and searches for a place to hide. I remember facts like this: The sperm whale has two tons of oil in its head.

★

Not long before, I was in a room crowded with Japanese businessmen, trying to think of a conversation topic. Everyone was locked behind their faces. Legs crossed. With a few well-rehearsed phrases, I maintained a discussion about traffic laws in Osaka while taking inventory of dress shoes, argyle socks, pocket translators, and eyelids that trapped emotion inside their heads.

★

We accelerate through the mountains in a white van. "Yes," I say, "sure," in response to the question she poses every day. She brings out the pita, hummus, cheese. To the right is a blue lake bounded by snowy mountains. We're in a hurry to get home to America. We're more in love than we've ever been. Lunchtime is like eating in outer space, orbiting. Years ago, I wanted badly to be alone, but I listened with envy to the parties next door.

We rip away the stale parts of the bread, fling them out the window. We eat in the van, speeding down the two-lane on the wrong side of the road, the ocean, the earth.

★

My brother rode in the back of a station wagon through the hills of northern Thailand. Beside him sat a prostitute. The prostitute's mother and father were in the front. My brother was dressed in new clothes that the hooker bought for him so he would look nice for her family.

My brother told me this story as we sipped beers in Bangkok. It made me jealous, but I didn't know why.

The next day, as our train rumbled south, I watched a diseased dog trot along a path beside the tracks. I wanted to shout that he was headed in the wrong direction, that there was nothing back there.

My wife, for the first time in her life, had short hair, cropped close like a boy's. My brother was on a plane to India; we were on our way to Malaysia. I was glad to be leaving the city. I never stopped trying to make something meaningful out of the smells, sounds, sights. I'm not sure I succeeded.

★

Two months later we're in an Auckland café, surrounded by white people once again after such a long time. Their skin is blotchy, red, chapped. I suppose ours is the same. More of me, more of her—more of all of this—awaits us in America.

My wife is sitting across from me, working hard at crossword puzzles. I pause in the middle of a daydream to tell her a four-letter word for exchange: Swap. I'm positive it's swap.

We've sold the van. We've booked the flight, packed the bags, and informed the families of our impending return.

Tonight there's a karaoke contest at the hostel across the street where we'll drink too much, make fools of ourselves, and fall, once again, just short of perfection.

Dangling Joe

You're a stranger now unto me
Lost in the dangling conversation.
And the superficial sighs,
In the borders of our lives.
—"The Dangling Conversation"

A man appeared as a speck against the clouds one morning, high above the city. The citizens were amazed and confused. From the ground they squinted, shielding their eyes. *Is that a person?* they asked. He was so distant he might as well have been a bag of rocks, which would have been equally amazing and confusing, floating in the air. However when witnesses produced binoculars and telescopes, they could distinguish him as a man. He was simply dangling in the sky. They searched above and below and beside him, seeing no wires, no platforms, and no means of support.

Not one person who looked closely at this man would have described him as floating or levitating. With his head upward and his feet pointed toward earth, he was in a standing position. However, the way his legs swayed beneath him (hips swinging gently side-to-side), and the uncomfortable-looking way he held his arms akimbo, gave the distinct impression that an invisible force was holding him like a yo-yo on a string.

The man appeared to be of Asian descent. Speculations were Chinese or Korean, but nobody really knew for sure. Was this fact important? Did his ethnicity make any difference? Maybe, maybe not. People yelled at each other in social media forums about it, criticizing those who noticed or questioned his ethnicity, criticizing those who said it didn't matter.

Nonetheless, nobody knew where he came from or what he was doing. His photo dominated all media outlets, yet no one came forth to identify him. He was dressed in an expensive-looking business suit, dark gray with subtle pinstripes. His polished loafers sparkling in the sunlight had been one of the first things that caught the attention of the folks on the ground. Chubby cheeks and a nicely combed head of conservatively parted hair rounded out his appearance. Aside from a bit of forehead perspiration sighted by an amateur astronomer, the man seemed untroubled by his bizarre and terrifying situation. His quiet smile exuded contentment and even joy as his legs rocked limply in the sky.

The city whirled into action. Emergency personnel—firefighters, police, paramedics—arrived at the area below him. Crowds gathered, shouting words of encouragement. They snapped photos, formed prayer circles, and set up hot dog carts. On rooftops of tall buildings, folks held signs that said *Don't fall!* and *We're here for you!* and *How are you dangling like that?* Even from the highest point in the city, the roof of a 47-story hi-rise apartment, the dangling man was too far to reach or hear. Not that he was talking or trying to communicate—he was just hanging there like laundry! The firefighters had no way to get to him. They needed a helicopter.

Cautiously and with great skill, the chopper pilot navigated near the man. He maneuvered until positioned thirty feet above. The rescuers unfurled a rope ladder, which flailed and flapped and whipped around until settling. *Grab it!* they shouted through a megaphone. Inexplicably, the man didn't respond. He didn't even crane his neck to look up at the chopper. His arms, though, were in a rather awkward position, which they figured made it tough to do much of anything. The poor guy!

A legendary search-and-rescuer by the name of Doc Ready hooked himself to a safety line and climbed down the ladder. In an acrobatic move, he slid his feet through the rungs and hung upside-down just above the man. Below, the crowd erupted into lusty cheers. What a hero! News reporters prepared the dramatic headlines: *Gutsy Rescue Dazzles Thousands of Onlookers*; *Courage in the Heavens*; *Noble Man Saves Helpless Other Man—Taxpayers Foot the Bill*.

But then an unexpected thing happened: The man simply moved, or was moved, sideways in the air, drifting like a leaf skidding along the pavement. He slowed to a stop about fifty yards from where he'd dangled originally. It looked like whatever was dangling him simply dragged him away with minimal effort.

This pissed off the rescuers, big-time. What the hell was going on? Doc Ready ascended the ladder. Carefully the pilot relocated the chopper, which took about eight minutes, since the winds were unpredictable at that altitude. They unfurled the ladder again. Doc clipped himself onto the safety line and descended, recreated his nifty little flip, extended his hand to the Asian man, listened to another burst of applause (more hesitant this time) from the ground.

The rescuers got the same result. Five more times they attempted the maneuver; five times the man slid away to a nearby location in the sky. By then the sun was setting. They were losing light.

"He doesn't speak. He doesn't acknowledge us. He hasn't been identified. Is he even an American? What evidence do we have that he's one of us?"

This was a pundit on one of the morning news shows, speaking angrily a couple of days after the man was first sighted. The pundit's name was Hank Hardwood. He was known for his powerful chin, piercing blue eyes, and scathing commentary about anyone he deemed un-American.

"How do we know he's not a spy for the Chinese government?" His face during this particular broadcast had lost its usual orange glow. In its place was a fiery red that practically emanated heat from people's TV screens. "He could have cameras and recording devices stuck everywhere on his body, sending classified information to his leaders, and here we are treating him like a damn hero!"

Normally this pundit talked so much that nobody paid attention to what he said. This time, however, people conceded that he might have a point. Wasn't this a national security issue? You couldn't just float above a city and expect not to get in trouble. And that smug little expression on his face—what was *that* all about? It seemed sneaky. And why were us taxpayers paying for these rescue attempts? Where was the FAA during all of this?

The FAA felt the pressure but could do nothing. Their federal aviation regulation stipulated that "over any congested area of a city, town, or settlement, or over any open air assembly of persons, an altitude of 1,000 feet above the highest obstacle within a horizontal radius of 2,000 feet of the aircraft—in this case, Joe—must be maintained." Dangling Joe (as the media had dubbed him) was within these limits and therefore doing nothing illegal. He wasn't harming anyone and didn't appear to be in any danger. Civil liberties groups quickly rallied to protect the man's right to dangle.

"You can get pulled over by the police for having an *air freshener* dangling from your rearview mirror," scoffed Hank Hardwood, "but you can't get in trouble for dangling from the *bleep-bleep* sky?"

"I think he's being remotely controlled," said one livid caller to Hank's show. "We all saw how he floated away from the rescuers! Somebody explain that to me!"

"How do we know he's not a weapon of mass destruction?" said another.

"I don't like his face," said another.

Society sorted into two distinct camps: 1.) Those who loved Dangling Joe, and 2.) Those who hated him. There was a third camp, too, but it was a pretty small camp. These people didn't love or hate Joe, but they wanted everyone to please recognize that he was *significant*. They were pretty sure he was a metaphor for something really interesting, and that's what they argued about, mostly at independent coffee shops.

T-shirts appeared with a picture of the man inside a red circle with a line through it: *Just Say No to Dangling Joe!*

Other shirts displayed Joe's beatific smile with the simple caption: *Joe Knows.*

Marry me, Joe! was another popular shirt.

The arguments intensified. Throngs of demonstrators, both pro- and anti-Joe, traveled from far corners of the country. They gathered beneath him to wave their signs and chant their chants. *Joe, Joe, you've got to go!* And *No Joe! No Joe!* And *Joe, Joe, he's our man, from Vietnam, China, or Japan! Yaaaay, JOE!* Security was overtaxed. Violence broke out. One guy chucked a rock at another guy, prompting a brawl. Hot dogs were stolen, car windows smashed. Someone was caught readying a high-powered rifle with a scope. The National Guard was deployed. The President issued a statement to Dangling Joe, delivered through a P.A. system in seven languages on a giant video screen set atop the 47-story building:

"Greetings, unknown man. This is the President of the United States. We don't know where you are from or what your purpose is. Nor do we know how you are dangling like that, defying gravity. We don't understand why you don't need food or water, nor why you look so pleased. Your presence, however, has caused us as a nation to do some serious self-reflection about our identity. Are we a country who welcomes strangers, whatever their origin, whatever their dangling preferences? Or are we distrustful and fearful of those who are different? Speak to us, dangling man! Tell us what to do. Remind us who we are."

The President broke down in tears. He was mocked for this roundly in the press. Some people liked his display of sensitivity, but most thought it showed weakness. Whether or not you were pro- or anti-Presidential tears, however, the undeniable result was that nobody talked about what the President had said. His message, his questions, his whole speech: ignored and forgotten. When his term expired, the President failed to even get his party's nomination for re-election.

The President's crying jag seemed to trigger the end of the mania. It's possible that he expressed some deep-seated feelings that citizens weren't even aware they had. Or that his tears represented the catharsis that the nation required in order to move on.

More likely, though, is the fact that even a phenomenon that breaks all known laws of physics gets boring after a while. People's necks got sore from staring up like that. They forgot he was there. What once seemed like a monumental moment in human history shrank to a blip on the radar of recorded time. The novelty of Dangling Joe soon wore off. Hank Hardwood set his sights on an outrageous new dance craze. Doc Ready, the man who'd come closest to Dangling Joe, stopped getting interviewed on talk shows. He died a couple of years later trying to rescue a moose trapped on a wayward block of ice. At his funeral he was remembered for the many people he had saved rather than the one man he hadn't.

I want to make it clear: Dangling Joe didn't go anywhere. He's still up there, if you look. But you've probably got more important things to do.

Three Men on a Boat

They began with hope. Piles of fish, they imagined, would fill the deck. Salmon, trout, sturgeon, pike, whatever they could get their hooks in. They weren't picky because they just loved being out on the open lake, together. Best buddies for many years, domestic obligations in the form of wives, children, and careers had made it practically fricking impossible to get together.

When are we going to do some fishing! they liked to write in emails, when they had the chance to email.

None of them could answer this question. Years passed. Their main way of staying in touch was checking out social media photos and observing the growth and accomplishments of each others' children: new teeth; cool rockets built and launched; awkward dance get-ups and big braces; regional volleyball tournaments; sunburns and crutches. They were proud of one another and couldn't believe how damn old they were all getting!

Once the children were out of high school and the wives had settled back into their careers and the men were in positions of authority at their jobs, granting them flexibility in choosing vacation dates, they finally found the time to go out and *get this thing done*.

The men all had quit smoking and cut back on (not quit!) drinking, but for this weekend they bought cigarettes and hard liquor and beer and agreed that this was going to be fucking fun. Christ, they'd earned it.

One of the men, whose name was Bill, owned the 30-foot fishing boat. Bill didn't like calling it a boat, however: he called it a *vessel*.

"This vessel's been good to me," he said when they boarded. "She's temperamental, though."

"Like all the women in your life, Billy," Carl joked.

"But what's up with the name?" Jack said.

The vessel was named *Huge Pen Is*.

"Don't like it?" Billy asked.

"I guess it's fine," Jack agreed.

Billy gave them a full tour: "10-inch Navnet, black box sounder, 600-watt transducer, hardtop outriggers, front and side curtains all up in here, fridge, stove, microwave, leg-mounted rod holders, sweet little cow pulpit, power steering, live well, toilet, sink, shower, stereo with satellite."

"You done good, Billy," the other men agreed.

After lunch at the dock they motored far out onto Lake Michigan. The sky was drawn with a stringy white cloud like a milk mustache on the face of God. Gentle waves swatted at the *Huge Pen Is* as it carved a path across the sparkling blue expanse. The wake trailed like a foamy serpent that would try and try but never quite overtake them.

"WOO!" Billy yelled, his hair windswept.

"WOO!" the other men answered.

They toasted with Styrofoam cups of Jack Daniels. The sun blazed high, naked and joyous. Forty miles out they dropped anchor and set their lines.

"Hope the cocksucking fish are biting," Jack said. At home he was careful not to use profanities. His wife didn't mind, but their wildly religious housekeeper found such language disturbing.

"Who cares either way," Carl said. "I'm just jacked to be out here with you guys. You're my dudes."

"Buds forever," Billy said.

"Buds," said Jack.

They drank another toast and a few more.

Hours passed with no bites. The boat rocked like a lazy cradle.

"This is so sweet," Carl said.

Many years—decades, really—had spread between the men, and yet such a comfort and familiarity remained that they felt no need to ask questions about careers, wives, children, television shows. They fell asleep in their seats under the warm sun.

Billy woke first. "Dang it, we missed the sunset," he said.

"Missed the sunset!" Jack screamed. He'd jolted awake and knocked his glass onto the deck, spilling a few gulps of Jack.

"We should prank Carl like we used to," Billy giggled.

They looked at Carl, who was snoring with his lips parted.

"Put something weird in his mouth," Jack suggested.

"I got a better idea. Let's flip him into the water."

"He can swim, can't he?"

"Used to be on the swim team if I remember correctly."

"Remember when they all shaved their heads and thought it was cool."

"Wasn't it cool?"

"I guess. Didn't impress me much."

"Got the girls all hot."

"Pff, girls."

"You grab that leg and I'll grab this one, and then whoopsy doo, he'll go flying out into the water."

"Hee hee."

"I can't believe we're doing this!"

"Hurry, he's waking up."

On the count of three Jack and Billy heaved. "He's too fat!"

They couldn't do much other than raise Carl a few inches off his seat. He woke up looking confused and irritated. Billy grabbed at his back. "Jeez, I popped something. Dammit, that hurt." He paced the deck, wincing and twisting.

"You guys trying to dump me?" Carl said groggily.

"If you weren't such a lardo you'd be in the water right now," Jack laughed.

"Good thing you didn't. I don't know how to swim."

"You weren't on the swim team?"

"No."

"We thought you were."

Billy started shouting and pointing as he hobbled toward the bow. "Bite! Bite!"

The tip of one of the rods was wiggling. Jack clambered to it, arriving ahead of Billy, and pulled the rod from its holder. He reeled and heaved, shoulders straining, leaning back and forward in a rhythmic action, the rod bent fiercely like a clawed finger.

"Bring that sucker in!" Carl clapped and hooted.

"Don't lose it, Jack."

Jack was huffing, cheeks tremoring with every breath. Sweat poured down his face. "Wipe me!" he cried, and Billy toweled his face like a welterweight trainer so his pal wouldn't have to stop the fight. Carl started snapping photos with his cell phone, but they were coming out pretty dark so he put his phone away.

The fish would not surrender. Jack refused to take a break. He needed to land this beast. He imagined the enormous mounted fish hanging triumphantly over his fireplace for many years. He imagined his two sons at his funeral, getting into a wrestling match as they argued over who would take possession of the beautiful salmon or whatever. He decided he would bequeath his trophy to the local library along with a donation so they would name a section of shelves after him.

"Holy crap, your face is red," Billy said. He was now seated, tired from watching and waiting, drowsy from the booze, a little angry that this was taking so long. What the heck time was it, anyway?

Just when Jack thought he might keel over, he felt the fish relent. "Get the net!" he cried.

Carl reached into the water, netted the fish, and laid it on the deck between them. It was a lake trout, twelve or thirteen inches.

"That's the fish?" Jack said. He thought surely his overheated, dehydrated brain was hallucinating. "No way is that the fish."

"Critter put up a valiant battle."

"Hope we can all say the same when it's our time."

"Want a picture with you holding it?"

"I can hardly breathe."

"God, would you look at this?" Carl said. "Guys!" He opened his arms wide as if to encompass the boat, the lake, the starry canopy, the moon's gentle eye, and the men themselves within and a part of it all.

"So sweet," Billy agreed.

Jack only nodded, perspiring, a weary smile tenuous on his face. He was either fading into a calm, easy sleep...or dying. At the moment he didn't care which.

"Guess I ought to guide this vessel back to shore," Billy said.

Billy started the engine and raised the anchor. Jack was softly belching.

"What if the shore isn't there anymore?" Carl asked after a few minutes.

"Guess we'd get a lot more fishing in," Billy said.

"Look around," Carl continued. "We can't see land. Yet we assume that it's there."

Billy rearranged his crotch while steering with the other hand.

"I'm throwing this guy back in the water," Jack announced. He'd regained his composure. With grunting effort he stood, de-hooked the trout, and held it. A profound fishy odor ascended into his nose. He drew a breath to fill his lungs and then, with a loud battle cry, reached back and hucked the fish like he used to huck footballs back in the day. His coach used to tell him he had a pro-ball-type arm. The trout sailed out into the darkness so far that he couldn't hear the splash. For a few moments Jack stood facing the water, tears brimming.

The sun was a glowing orange line on the horizon as the *Huge Pen Is* reached the marina.

Seagulls hovered along the beach, a light breeze caressed. Classic rock grooved on the radio. A perfect morning.

Pleasantly exhausted, sweaty, and slightly drunk, the men disembarked. Their flip-flops slapped against the dock as the gear-laden men made their way to their cars. Alone in the parking lot and miles from all responsibility, they embraced each other, promising to do this again really fucking soon.

Festivity

When guests cross the threshold they will believe they are entering the mouth of a living beast.

They will breathe the sweet odor of their fallen ancestors on the ceiling fan breeze. They will comprehend the porousness of skin.

The walls will be operatic, the floors imperial. The ceiling will evoke the star-loud night.

In every corner of every room, shining towers of scotch, bourbon, vodka, and gin will rise like cities.

Jazz will ooze from wall-mounted speakers, suggesting the primordial pleasures of lower-order microorganisms.

Festivity

Mouths will gnash the shrimp cocktail, crab-stuffed mushrooms, pickled herring, and velvety ropes of asparagus. Lips glistening with garlic and oil. Erotic grunts of mastication singing in the air. Gurgles of joy, the random slurp of contentment. Gastrointestinal flirtations erupting moistly between strangers. Loins poetically stirred like plains grasses swept by hot wind.

Guests wordlessly compelled to make paintings using each other's tears. Impromptu magic tricks with names like The Unbendable Rope, The Dishcloth Apparition, and The Font of Regret.

Arm wrestling. Leg wrestling. Neck wrestling. Catapult competitions. Ten-meter crawls through pig waste beneath blankets of electrified wire. Shirtless husking. Sweat lodges constructed under the dining room table, prompting vision quests. Re-enactments of famous film scenes. Spontaneous auctions, selling hindsight and other useless skills.

The night will stretch like a balloon filling with water. The night will grow so large, so bulbous and taut, that onlookers will cringe in expectation of explosion.

But inevitably, quietly, the sun will rise, ushering the darkness to its hidden corners. Revelers will blink as if waking from a dream. In silence they will gather their belongings, avoiding each other's glances, abashed by the intimacies of the night. Into the morning air they will depart.

They will return to their ordinary lives. Drywall ceilings, scuffed sneakers, plain corn chips.

Hours will pass. Days, months, and years. Memories of the festivities will shrink, becoming gauzy and dry like cobwebs. Now and then will they spot a mirror or a window and see the ghosts they left behind.

Sunlight and sunset will mark the end and beginning of nothing but sleep.

And then one day, their trembling hand will reach into the mailbox. An envelope. An invitation.

Possibilities and Considerations

STORY:

An American woman climbs Mt. Everest with the help of two male Sherpas. At the summit, she stares out over the majestic cloud-swept vista, a panorama that clears, momentarily, the storm inside her. The sunset casts a mauve blanket across the mountains like the work of some divine paintbrush. Nearby the Sherpas are setting up camp, speaking in loud voices and laughing. They have done this journey many times, and have seen this view before. In her thick parka, hat and gloves, the woman is warm. She feels the enormity of the moment and her own smallness within it and can almost hear the voice of her dead husband saying her name on the wind. She smiles at the triteness of this idea, but her heart feels hushed and content. At night she sleeps undisturbed, except for one moment when she wakes to the soft grunts of her Sherpas having sex in the adjoining tent.

STORY:

A pickle is stolen from the White House kitchen. The news breaks on a Monday morning, and everyone assumes it's an off-season April Fool's joke. But no, they're serious. A press conference announces the theft of the Presidential pickle. The press secretary, a young man with prematurely gray hair and an intensely puckered mouth, stares into the camera and says, "The pickle was last seen yesterday afternoon, nestled in a jar with other pickles of its kind. We have no further information." He is obviously restraining a storm of emotion, which whirls and billows beneath his twitchy façade. The missing pickle is a dagger to his heart. "The President will ask Congress to approve a full-scale search," he continues, "including the deployment of the National Guard, and is seeking every citizen's help in retrieving this important pickle." The screen shows an artist's rendering of the pickle. The audience of television and Internet viewers has been eagerly awaiting this visual because there's been some confusion about what the pickle looks like, what sort of pickle they're supposed to be finding: Is it a chip? A spear? One of those fat dills that barely fits in your mouth? It is none of these. The technical term is a "sweet midget," although these days "midget" is considered insensitive, so the press secretary avoids this word when describing it. But in the drawing it's pretty obvious that's what it is. It's a curved, warty little thing, swampy green. There's a scale on the side of the drawing, making the picture resemble a mug shot. The pickle is two inches long, maybe two and a half. Still, the nation understands that this is serious. The press covers the story 24 hours a day. The citizens live in a state of anxiety and instability as local and federal personnel are deployed to cities, towns, villages, and burgs. The Great Pickle Hunt, as it will come to be known, does not have a happy ending. It does not have a resolution. It continues to this day.

STORY:

Three babies love each other. No words are necessary between them. They merely sit on a cotton blanket together, spilling drool onto each other's tummies and thighs, gingerly extending hands to touch soft bare skin. Diapered and dry, they are exceedingly happy. Angled sunlight warms their square of fabric, the precious space that is their world. They cannot walk or crawl or feed themselves, but in each other's glowing smiles they see themselves shining back at them, and that is enough.

STORY:

A man with a crossbow storms into a fast-food restaurant and starts screaming. He isn't making any sense at all. Something about cattle feed and biomedical ethics and the cost of repairing America's roadways? The crossbow is being waved threateningly above his head, which looks like a terrorist explosion all on its own with its nest of gnarled hair. A beard has overtaken the man's face, leaving visible only a potato-shaped nose and two burning black eyes that seemingly want to leap out of his skull. While his head appears enormous (an effect of his overlarge hair), his body looks shrunken in his saggy flannel and corduroys. He may or may not have feet; they aren't visible under long pants that drape the floor. One of the fast food employees tells the man he's not allowed to have a crossbow in the restaurant, and could he please take it outside? This is a sturdy white-haired woman who appears easily capable of hurtling the counter and wrestling this dude to the ground. The customers give the man his space by running out the doors. They aren't interested in his pleas and questions. They'll take their chances at the fast food place across the street. For a moment the man looks hurt and lost, as the doors swing closed and he realizes that his audience has abandoned him. In fact, now it is only him and the white-haired woman, who stares at him with demanding eyes, challenging him. He points the crossbow at her and makes his final plea.

STORY:

Rain. So much rain. Even when the clouds are gone and the sky is clear and blue, it rains. Fungus grows on the skin of humans. Flood-related deaths happen so frequently that they're boring. The constant sizzle and patter on rooftops and pavement convinces an entire generation that silence is the sound of rain.

STORY:

A robin stands on the edge of the ceramic fire-pit circle, orange-breasted, head darting left and right at inquisitive angles. Her trills go unanswered. Lawnmowers buzz. Wind moves the flag hung from the garage, but not enough for a full flap, so it sways in a perfunctory way. A quiet afternoon, as seconds tick by. A woman is raped by her close friend. A car alarm sounds. Two squirrels chase along a branch. A boy makes an outstanding catch in left field, sliding in the grass and coming up with the ball in his glove, beaming.

STORY:

The production of this story that you are reading now is made into a major motion picture. The protagonist is a Caucasian man in his early forties, and he spends the duration of the movie sitting at a table, typing on his laptop. Much attention is given to close-ups of his fingers as they work the keyboard, the tap-tap-tap of each letter amplified and booming in the dynamic Dolby Surround Sound. The furrowed brow, haunted eyes, and clenched jaw of the protagonist also feature quite prominently in the film. The actor who plays "the writer" (the only appellation given to this character) is actually quite a bit older than his early forties, but he was hired because his age lends him an air of gravitas and profundity that the producers feel doesn't truly exist in forty-year-old men of this generation. "We need to believe that this guy could write these stories," one of the producers says, or said, when the group was initially flipping through headshots and making their deliberations. "He has to carry a felt sense of a life lived," said another, emphasizing the phrase *felt sense*, enjoying the feel of it on her tongue. Production of the film takes seven weeks, shot in Toronto. Box office returns on the movie are disappointing, and it is ignored during awards season. However, a few positive reviews call it "whimsical and without fear" and "a wild and despairing journey."

Session 2

Q: If you had three wishes, what would they be?

A: The first would be the ability to fluently speak any language on earth. The second wish would be that nobody would ever understand a word I said, no matter what I said, no matter what language I was speaking. My third wish would be to change my first wish. The third wish would allow me to re-wish my first wish, revising it so that *everybody* would understand *everything* I said, in whatever language I was speaking. Having two opposing wishes like this—how could that be possible? The genie's head would probably explode, and I would snap a picture of that.

Q: When your second wish was granted, that would mean that the genie wouldn't understand any ensuing statements you made. Therefore, he (let's say the genie is male) would not be able to grant your third wish since it would be incomprehensible.

A: I would write it on a notepad.

Q: Do you remember much about that Saturday?

A: I woke up with a raging sore throat and a horrible case of sticky-eyes. Allergies. They were pretty terrible that year in general, not in a seasonal way, just constantly. My state of mind was *Why me? Is this a punishment for the girls I slept with and never called again?* So I made an appointment, went to the doctor, endured the battery of tests, you know those little pokey pricks up and down your back? They tested me for nine hundred and fifty-five thousand irritants, something like that. Turns out I was allergic to one thing: *tree*. That's what the allergist said. "You came back positive for tree." *Positive for tree?* Who could make this stuff up? After that, whenever I walked up and down the block I noticed towering trees, trees I hadn't even realized existed. They were everywhere! And they looked sinister, stalking in yards and on corners with faces curled up in the bark, malicious, mocking me and sneering like, "Hahaha, you idiot, what are going to do, chop us all down? Get used to your eyes being glued shut and your head full of gunk because we're gonna crush you." What choice did I have? I couldn't live in Michigan anymore, no way. I left my wife and children and moved to the desert. Took up pottery-making and sold bowls, vases, and cream and sugar holders on the side of the highway. The heat was wretched, like being stepped on by the devil's heel. A few layers of my skin burned off within the first hour. Eventually I purchased a tent and that helped a bit.

Q: That's quite a lot for one Saturday.

A: It was the '90s.

Q: The law of averages says that you'll be unhappy at some point in your life. Generally the feeling of happiness has the effect of producing other, more contradictory feelings, such as guilt and fear—the fear that the happiness will end, which naturally it does when the fear overtakes the happiness as the primary emotion. Therefore the sadness becomes a kind of self-inflicted emotion, which of course is no less impacting than sadness inflicted by circumstances beyond your control. You could conjecture by this logic that the sadness, once accepted, would be followed easily by happiness, since you will have performed your "sadness duty" so to speak and should no longer feel guilty about being happy, or fearful that the happiness will end. However, it seems that it doesn't work that way. These feelings of sadness create other equally contradictory emotions, such as wishing unhappiness upon others—the old "misery loves company" idea—or fear that the happiness will never return, which again is the self-inflicted variety, by the way, or guilt that your own unhappiness can never match the unhappiness of those who've suffered legitimate trauma, and—

A: Confusion.

Q:

A: Yes, confusion as an emotion. That's what I feel when I talk to you. Not that you are confusing in particular. But in general, yes. I think about the word itself, the root obviously being *fusion*, to join together two or more objects; or in this case, concepts. And the suffix *con* means *against*. So con-fusion exists when the concept or event or whatever doesn't successfully join with your mind, with your perceptions or understanding. Personally, I walk around in a persistent state of confusion about numerous aspects of life, especially people. Their reactions, their words and mannerisms, their beliefs, their taste in music and entertainment, their clothing, their ability to believe in God and the afterlife, their acceptance of mediocrity in every field except sports. All of this leaves me in a state of confusion at all times, and this confusion makes me sad. Confusion as emotion.

Q: You speak of people using the pronoun "they." Do you consider yourself a person?

A: I'll let history define who or what I was.

Q: How much time is enough time?

A: Usually a couple of minutes.

A Fine Time

I asked her how long I would have to wait like this, tied to the bed.

She said *a while* and left the room.

I stared at the ceiling, thinking about snow. I hadn't seen snow in 600 years, give or take. When I was a kid it was my life. Michigan blizzards, ice storms, sledding, snowmobiling with Mom and Dad. That was all so long ago that it seemed like another person's story.

Thinking about snow made the room seem chilly. I actually felt a draft on my testicles. Probably she turned on the air conditioning, or I was having a stroke. She rarely used the air conditioning. She enjoyed seeing me sweat.

I heard the whir of a blender or a food processor. Was she making me a margarita? Doubtful. I loved margaritas. I smelled garlic and guessed guacamole. The girl knew how to tease. My stomach rumbled.

My boner was long gone. I assured myself it would return.

But what if it didn't? Sometimes when we finished having sex I would contemplate this possibility. Maybe this was the last time I would feel myself inside her, feel myself firming up like that, all of my blood rushing to that sweet spot. I fucking loved boners. Even on other dudes they looked fine. For my money, boners were the purest physical manifestation of desire in the world, and who could argue with that?

When a person lost his desire, what did he have left?

TV. TV and death.

I wished she had turned on the TV before she walked out.

D.T. Myse's *Cold Blood from a Scorched Cat: Sweet Whiskers in the Grip of Death*

Book Review by Olsen Giles White

Upon first encountering D. T. Myse's debut novel, a reader's initial reaction will likely be confusion and disgust. The publisher's decision to leave the cover blank—front, back, and spine absent of title, author, or publication information—will be viewed with one of two responses: 1.) "I wonder what might be inside this burlap monstrosity?" or the more likely 2.) "I'd just as soon open that Tupperware that's been in my fridge for seven months."

Continuing with the confusion (while segueing into the disgust), the sheer size of the hardcover tome will be noted. This reviewer is not in the habit of keeping a tape measure at the ready, but when set against the length of his size-12 feet, Myse's book easily extends three or four inches beyond. And the width is identical! Yes, this is a gigantic square book. Buyers be warned: Put your local carpenter on speed-dial so he can hammer out a new bookshelf just to accommodate this literary Sasquatch.

And how lengthy is this enormous tome, you ask? Believe me, this reviewer would love to share that information. However, since the publisher elected to omit page numbers, counting would be a ridiculous, tedious task. Let's just say it's girthier than a Manhattan telephone book. Thicker than a ½ pound hamburger (bun included).

But please don't eat this burger: As the pages are flipped, one will notice a mild but persistent odor fogging the air. At the onset, one may (as did this reviewer) attribute the scent to one's own environment—apartment, alley, yurt, wherever you prefer to enjoy the wonders of language—or to gastrointestinal distress.

Make no mistake, the scent ("stench" is too strong of a word, but "scent" isn't quite right either) is subtly overpowering, and is indeed emanating from Myse's novel. The odor has a chemical quality, bleach-like, bearing hints of almond and talcum powder, a complex bouquet that is yeasty, dense, and acidic, calling to mind rye bread bathed in turpentine. The effect is disarming, to say the least. It is not recommended to open this book while driving a motor vehicle or operating heavy machinery. In fact, do not open it around other people. Be alone in a well-ventilated room, preferably beside a window in case you begin to feel light-headed (you will). Those of you required by waning health to use supplemental oxygen tanks may in fact be Myse's ideal reader.

For this reviewer, the reading experience was underwhelming in the literary sense. It may have been a result of the powerful fumes, but Myse's sentences—indeed, each word—swam and danced upon the page in a hypnotic and disorienting fashion, triggering a response just shy of chunder. More than once the book fell to the floor with a resounding thud as this reader belched and swooned, besotted by migraines. Every reader's experience is different, naturally, and there is no telling whether this will happen to you.

However, it must be acknowledged that we critics search far and wide for books that provide a visceral experience. Grudgingly: Myse's tome fits this criterion, despite the fact that what populates the pages is not memorable. No single word, character, or plot point calls itself to mind when reflected upon. The reading experience was rather like being put under sedation during surgery: dreamy, anxious, and swirling with unsettling images of vermin streaming like water from the walls.

One thing is certain: Myse's novel is not the "lighthearted romp," nor the "wise and nuanced journey," nor the "spectacle of whimsy and magic reminiscent of a child's first day at the beach"; neither is it "sublimely sweet, like being dipped into chocolate sauce and licked into ticklish frenzy by a bevy of bunnies" like the blurbers so gushingly contend. One wonders if we even received the same book!

Some consideration must also be given to the voices.

They whisper while I drift into sleep: sweet sibilance in the darkness near my head. Voices neither man nor woman, yet somehow both. The mouse fears the beast with sweetness on his whiskers. Beguiling words, issued like a threat. Upon opening my eyes, nobody is in the room. I am alone and cold.

Weeks later, the odor has not dissipated (despite repeated airing and cleansing).

The book's cover has grown mildew, freckled with jaundiced spores. In time, the mold will certainly spread to other books, and then to the carpet, bed, and kitchen.

This reviewer's body will likely follow. Already the skin of his hands and forearms are showing faint discoloration.

Each touch of Myse's tome releases a delicate, vaporous puff, eagerly inhaled. Regular food is no longer necessary.

Visitors to this reviewer's home (he hasn't left the apartment in weeks, perhaps longer) express a grotesque jealousy of his circumstances. Each demands a private viewing with Myse's novel, but that will not be allowed. Their knocks are less frequent with each passing day.

And so, poised in full view of the flimsy membrane between worlds, this reviewer will proclaim his final judgement:

A full four-star rating. Repeat readings recommended. Repeat readings recommended. Afull fourstarr ating.

Afullfourst arr ating.

A fullf ourst arra ting

Second Home

Weiland felt wrong, all wrong. In the waiting room of the Oral Revitalization Office he dropped heavily into his throne-like ES Chair. The world dimmed around the corners of his vision; his body swooned. An impulse told him to put his head between his knees, which was a position he'd never assumed before. The ES Bowl automatically lowered into the region where his skull was supposed to be, but Weiland's bent posture left it hanging empty above him.

The other patients awaiting Oral Revitalization cast sidelong glances at Weiland. Their heads were ensconced in clear plastic domes that provided a near-infinite variety of viewing and listening options, from Mandroid Bowling Tournaments to Virtual Crater Hikes to

My Favorite Singing Mandroid. Still, these other patients—an advanced woman who looked to be in her 17th decade; a man like Weiland, approximately mid-journey age; and a little girl with her pregnant mother—all appeared interested in Weiland's plight. Not interested enough to ask him if he needed help; this would require removing the ES Bowl, which could be painful and messy if done too hastily.

The waiting room was not large to the naked eye, consisting of a dozen cushioned Entertainment Station Chairs, a dozen wall-mounted cotton ball dispensers, two yellow and pink potted plant-like decorations, and a jumbo LED screen where Weiland had performed his digital check-in with the virtual receptionist. However, if Weiland had been willing and able to walk to his right or to his left, he would keep walking for a half-mile, passing through other waiting rooms, an uninterrupted chain of rooms exactly like this one, before arriving again at his ES Chair. District M-17's ORO, like all MPCs (Mortality Prevention Centers), was a free-floating circular structure hovering 100 meters above the earth. Waiting rooms ringed the perimeter, while the procedure rooms were located in the center.

Normally Weiland enjoyed wearing the ES Bowl. In each of the dozens of waiting rooms that made up his and everyone's life, from the Skin Re-Graphing to the Retinal Refurbishing to the Organ Maximization to the Fingerprint Etching to the Colon and Bowel Salvage to the Bone Cleanser, patients were politely asked to connect to their ES Bowls and experience a wide array of amusement options while awaiting replenishment. In a typical week most people visited two or three MPCs, and Weiland was no exception. Spending an hour in an ES Bowl was never unpleasant, except for the occasional nosebleed, which was not enough of a nuisance to cause pain or alarm. The cotton ball dispensers made quick work of staunching them.

Today, however, Weiland couldn't connect to his ES Bowl. He was paralyzed, swooning beneath the power of the buzzing sensation that raged through his body. It was the nearest he'd felt to death in all of his 93 years, and the worst discomfort by far. Sweat broke out on his forehead. When he touched his skin he recoiled in disgust at the wetness on his fingers.

The world had been meticulously designed to enable people to live two hundred years without pain, strife, or perspiration. Diseases were eradicated or easily treatable. Body parts were exchanged and fixed, cleaned and maintained. Most people didn't have jobs, the exceptions being the politicians, scientists, and (Weiland presumed) the cotton ball factory workers. Mandroids and Virtual Receptionist technicians handled the bulk of the labor. They were ubiquitous and efficient. They usually had decent senses of humor, too, to keep things light. Transportation pods moved people from one MPC to another and then back to their houses. Groceries were delivered; yard work was unneeded because there were no yards. Life consisted of remaining unstressed and pleasant at all times. Eating, sleeping, fornicating, participating in the Global Health Imperative, and sitting with heads in ES Bowls: these were the Sweet Fruits of the Mandroid Revolution.

Safe and Breathing, Creating Memories was the slogan Weiland had grown up hearing within the ES Bowl and reading on sky-flung billboards. *Safe and breathing*, his mom and dad used to say before kissing his forehead and watching with dewy eyes as the sleeping tube inserted itself into the rear of his brain pan.

★

Thirty minutes before his scheduled appointment, the virtual receptionist blinked to life on the screen and called Weiland's name. He managed to stand shakily and enter the procedure room, which slid open with a welcoming *ding!*

The Mandroid Dentist, a fine-looking man with curled blond hair, an athletic body, and an arresting smile, greeted him with a firm handshake. Every Mandroid's physical traits were modeled on one of the earth's most populous segments: Asiopean or, in this Dentist's case, Floridian. Despite their appellation, Mandroids were not all men. But female Mandroids, like their male counterparts, had no genitalia or orifices below the belt. If they were ever forced to engage in sexual activity, they were programmed to vomit acid.

"Your vitals were looking a bit distressed," the Dentist said with an optimistic lilt to his voice. "Figured I'd get you in ahead of the others and make sure you're A-OK."

Weiland, like all people, had sensors implanted in his body that could be accessed and analyzed, networked to the Mandroids. He'd never met this particular Dentist before; he rarely saw the same Mandroid twice.

Weiland's History Capsules, required viewing in his early days, had told of a time when there were human nurses and other nonessential personnel employed at places like this facility. Streamlining the service industry was another of the Sweet Fruits, freeing up humans to spend more time at home with their food and their ES Bowls.

The Dentist told Weiland to have a seat, gesturing toward the examination chair.

"Your pulse rate was elevated, your breathing was erratic. You came close to losing consciousness. These are the symptoms of a severe panic attack."

"Is that a disease?" Weiland felt his heartbeat speed up again. The sensation was uncomfortable, shaking his insides. Was losing consciousness the same as dying?

"Not a disease. Panic attacks are a gumbo of not-nice emotions: fear, worry, anxiety, and so on. It's not a condition we've seen in a while. Here, allow me to give you something."

The Dentist applied a sticky square patch to Weiland's neck. Immediately a wave of soothing sedation washed through him. His eyelids lowered and his breathing returned to normal.

"Today's visit is not an ordinary one," the Dentist said with excitement. "In fact, it's quite a special occasion. You'll be receiving a full extraction. As you've probably heard, we now are able to eliminate physical teeth altogether. This is a new procedure, but soon everyone will have it. You'll be the first on your grid."

Weiland felt dreamy and soft. This procedure room looked no different than every procedure room he'd visited since he was a child: white walls, cool shiny steel implements and big, imposing laser machines; a couple of electronic posters of waterfalls, mountains, and creatures from days of yore. By his conservative estimate he'd been to over 5,000 of these rooms in the past nine decades. They were like his second home. *Or maybe my first,* he thought sleepily.

"Virtual teeth are the wave of the future," the Dentist continued. "Once your physical teeth are removed, I will implant 32 microchips beneath the surface of your gums. These chips will project virtual teeth that look and feel exactly like your original teeth. You'll bite and chew like you always have. Except now you won't have to worry about cavities, decay, chipping, blah blah blah. You can throw away your toothbrushes and floss.

You can even disable the teeth and go full-gum when you want it. How cool is that?"

It sounded confusing to Weiland. He'd already thrown away his toothbrush and floss. Nobody had owned those things for years. With monthly dental visits that scoured and sculpted and polished and reinforced with immaculate precision, they just weren't necessary.

"These are nothing like the imitation teeth of two centuries ago," the Dentist said. He pressed a button that eased the chair back so that Weiland reclined, facing the ceiling, upon which was an animated tree blowing gently in a breeze. "False teeth, they were called. Pretty accurate name, if you ask me. Filling your body with lies, trying to fool you into believing you were still young. Those were stopgaps on the way to the grave. Thankfully, as you know, the grave is something you don't have worry about for quite some time. Or, if progress continues, ever." He offered a smile that seemed to convey love and affection touched with regret—regret that such an unsavory subject as death even needed to be discussed.

Through the fog of the sedative Weiland managed to say, "How can I chew with...teeth?"

He'd meant to insert the word *virtual*, but it had escaped him.

The Dentist chuckled and took a seat on the stool beside Weiland. The misty scent of orange sandalwood wafted to Weiland's nose. He felt the reassuring hand of the Dentist on his arm. The bedside manner of the Mandroids was impeccable.

"It's complicated. Pulses, lasers, ultrasonic sound waves, that's all you need to know. I'll handle the techno-babble. That's what they pay me for, right? But there's a pamphlet I will happily transmit to your ES Bowl."

"Why did I feel that way in the lobby?"

"The panic attack." The Dentist paused, perhaps scrolling his vast database for the most efficient phrase to soothe his patient. "Frankly, it used to be a fairly common problem. Trips to the dentist were especially scary, or so I've heard. Not true today, as you know." He nodded, again patting Weiland's arm. "I suspect if you'd gotten connected to your ES Bowl right away it wouldn't have happened."

"But what..." His mind struggled through the haze. "...what...caused it?"

The Dentist seemed to consider the question, his jaw set and expression pensive. His baby blue eyes sparkled under the mellow glow of the spectrometric lights. "Primitive impulses and instincts. It's quite amazing. They linger. Despite the efforts from our scientists to keep people happy, these primitive impulses still pop up now and then. Wired deep, I suppose. But mostly we—or I should say *you*—are beyond those."

The world was becoming distant, but Weiland concentrated, holding on. He wanted to know: "What impulses? What stinks?" He was trying to say *instincts*.

"The biological instinct to survive. Back in the old days, survival sometimes depended on emotions like fear, sadness, worry: that whole mess. Thankfully you don't need to concern yourself with those feelings anymore. Safe and breathing. Now rest your eyes, and in a jiffy you'll be right as rain."

Weiland was drifting off. He began to dream, half-awake, half-asleep. He imagined microchips implanted under his scalp, sprouting virtual hair. He saw microchips in his torso; his arms and legs being gently amputated and replaced with projections of arms and legs, hands and feet. And then, sure, his head. Soon microchips would project Weiland's whole body—his whole self—in perfect form. He saw his mom and dad, grandparents and great-grandparents, aunts and uncles, cousins, nieces, nephews, and friends. Every person he had known and could know, none of them physical bodies but all of them whole, created in exquisite human image: eternal. He saw his flesh and blood body whittled away piece by piece, trimmed by the wonders of advancement, replaced by projections that would never fail, his virtual heart pumping virtual blood, his virtual eyes shimmering with joy as he greeted his virtual face in the virtual mirror, the pulsating tectonics of the universe thrumming within him, the electronic impulses of love and desire and—

Faintly and from a great distance he heard the wet cracking of his roots ripping free.

The Search for Boyle

Five workdays and two weekends had passed and none of us had seen Boyle. Hadn't seen him at the plant, hadn't seen him at Curly's, hadn't seen him around town walking his cat. Hadn't seen him and he wasn't answering his phone. He didn't have a phone, so this wasn't surprising. But he did have a house, and when we knocked on the front door he didn't answer. Mail was stuffed in the box like it hadn't been touched for a while, except probably by the postal carrier.

From what we'd ascertained in our dealings with him, Boyle had no family in town or nearby. Mickel thought it was a good idea to bust inside and see if he'd died. Seemed like the right plan, so we kicked in the back door, broke the door jam and really distressed the wood on the door itself.

The Search for Boyle

We examined the damage and promised if he was alive we would get it fixed for him.

The place seemed empty. Empty of Boyle, anyway. We called out his name without reply. His stuff was where it always was, or where we assumed it always was. None of us had been in his house before. We didn't know him well. Nobody did. He was a quiet sort even though he did come out to Curly's every Friday night. But he generally sat and listened and drank his beer and kept half his attention on the TV, no matter what was playing.

His possessions stood in orderly, expected positions: kitchen table in the kitchen, couch and TV in the living room, coffee maker on the counter. The man lived a very basic existence. The TV, for example, had a 12-inch screen, and aside from the possessions just named there wasn't much else in the house. The bathroom had a few toiletries on the counter and toilet paper under the sink. One bedroom was totally empty, dust bunnies dancing across the wooden floor when we made a breeze by walking in. The other room, presumably his bedroom, had a single mattress, no bed frame. The top sheet and blanket were twisted around each other, and the pillowcase had drool stains. A trumpet stood on its bell in the corner. That was the weirdest thing; that trumpet in the corner. We all pictured Boyle up late at night, reclining on his mattress, eyes wet with drink, blowing bluesy licks under a bare yellow bulb. It was such a lonely picture that we shook it away fast.

In the fridge were a few condiments and a pack of American cheese. In the freezer, a near-empty box of fish sticks.

"Maybe he went grocery shopping," Mickel said.

Phil said, "Suppose it would take a week to get what he needed."

We laughed. Then we heard the low growling.

In the basement was his cat. When we opened the door, the beast bolted through the kitchen and disappeared around the corner. It was probably all crazed and starving.

Boyle's cat was no ordinary cat. It was a crossbreed, half domestic and half African Serval. It was a long tall son-of-a-bitch, lean and muscular with jumbo ears, its light brown fur patterned with cloud-shaped spots like a tree or a fish. That's why Boyle had to walk it on a leash.

The cat wasn't mean or anything. Just kept to itself and wasn't fond of being touched. No way could Boyle let it roam like a regular outdoor cat, and no way could he leave it inside all day. Probably if it didn't release its feral energy it would eat him. Or at least chew him.

This idea made us wonder if Boyle had been devoured. Was his body in the basement? Did the hybrid get hungry and overpower him?

"Where is the animal's food?"

We descended the staircase. The lighting made us feel like we had cataracts. The chilly air smelled like pine boards, soil, urine, and feces. Must and dust hung thick. It was an old-fashioned Michigan basement: a single room with ancient wood shelving constructed against stone retaining walls. Cobwebs. Dirt floors. No Boyle body, mercifully. Two empty metal bowls lay upended, the crusted remnants of old meat clinging to the sides of one of them. In the corner near the furnace was a jumbo plastic tub filled with litter and clumpy excrement. An explosion of litter surrounded the tub.

"Kitty definitely sprayed down here," Burt said, squeezing his nose like he wanted to tear it off.

"Hey, look at that." Mickel was pointing to one of the shelves.

We saw what he saw: a camera. Not a super-new model, but new enough to be digital.

"Why would he keep a camera in the basement?"

"Maybe he left it by accident."

"We may need Sheriff Cole."

"Yeah, this is Boyle's property."

"We busted into his house," I said. "That point is moot."

We took the camera upstairs and sat at the kitchen table. Mickel poked around in the cupboards while we tried to decide what to do.

"Apparently Boyle's not a complete loser," Mickel said after a minute. He'd found a near-full fifth of Canadian whisky.

We passed around the bottle. Outside the window night was in full bloom. Although nobody said it aloud, we felt like we were steeling ourselves against some big dark revelation.

The Search for Boyle

Nobody wanted to look at the pictures, but at the same time we knew we would.

"Let's talk this through," Burt said.

"His keys and wallet ain't here," Mickel said.

"No sign of forced entry."

"Except ours."

"Hang on. Where's his car?"

"In the shop," Phil said. "I was down there today to get mine serviced. It's still there."

"So he didn't take a trip."

"Unless someone else drove him."

"He have any friends?"

"Just us."

"Maybe a secret girlfriend."

"You ever *seen* Boyle?"

"You should talk."

We drank for a while, the camera poised in the center of the table like a forbidden relic out of a fairy tale: the object that should never be touched, the door that shouldn't be opened. None of us wanted to make a move. Because if that camera held something terrible, it would feel like whoever looked first was the one to let it into the world.

Burt startled in his chair. "Whoa. You scared me, buddy."

The cat was perched on the counter behind Mickel's head, staring at us.

"Should we go buy some cat food?"

"Maybe kitty wants whisky."

Phil brought out a bowl, poured a bit of the sauce into it, and set it on the counter.

"Wasteful."

"Hang on, maybe not."

Sure enough, the hybrid was licking away at the hooch.

"I'll be damned."

"Someone ought to take a picture of that."

We all had phones with cameras, but the mention of photography brought us back to the dilemma at hand.

"Christ, what are we waiting for?" Mickel said. He grabbed the camera and turned it on. It beeped. We all gathered around to stare at the little display screen.

The first photo was of Boyle himself, sitting on his mattress with the trumpet pressed against his lips, pretty much exactly how we'd imagined him. I could almost hear the sad wail of that horn calling for the angels. He had a look in his eyes like a man about to go into major surgery or jump off a cliff.

"Who do you suppose took this picture?" Burt asked.

"That could be a clue."

But the second photo was a bigger surprise than the first. It was a close-up of me in Boyle's basement, my eyes squinted in a quizzical fashion, stooped and staring into the lens.

"Where'd that cat go?" Mickel asked.

The third photo was Burt taking a sip from a bottle of Canadian whisky.

The fourth was Phil peering into a cupboard, wearing a wry smile, gripping a bowl.

The fifth was Mickel reaching toward the camera, mouth open like he was caught mid-statement, like he was about to turn the thing on.

"We're all seeing this, right?" Phil asked. Nobody answered out loud; we were holding our breaths and our thoughts as tight as possible because the rest of the world felt like it was slipping away.

The sixth picture was of the cat, its face buried in a pile of raw pink meat.

There weren't any more pictures.

"Where is that cat?"

"I don't know. Where's Mickel?"

We looked around. We didn't remember him leaving.

"Did Phil go look for him?"

"Not that I can recall."

"Burt? You still here?"

"Guys?"

I didn't remember going down to the basement, but that's where I found myself. Had I come down here to look for my friends? Why hadn't I turned on a light?

I stood in the cold blackness breathing the soil and the urine and something else, something rich and metallic. I called out for my friends. Wherever they were, they weren't with me. Neither was Boyle, nor anybody else.

It was me, the darkness, and the chewing. Just the wet hungry insistence, teeth on flesh, and the hot, wild stink of that goddamn cat.

Party Town

The party never stopped at Party Town. No matter the hour, day, or season, music blared from homes and apartments, where people danced and booze flowed. Classic rock, house beats, country, Latin jazz—whatever your taste, the only rule was to crank that shit. Solo cups littered lawns, sprinkled like red candies amid cornhole boards, sofas, and beer pong tables. Folks wandered the streets, house to house, searching for more and finding it. Old, young, black, white, fat, thin—they were all invited and they all came. Little kids zipped around, playing tag as their parents got wasted. For as long as anyone could remember it had been this way. They were exhausted, sure, but having a ton of fun. Sleep was allowed if you needed it, which everyone eventually did, but they all got used to nodding off to the thump of bass and the squeals of happy revelers.

They'd heard about other towns where people had jobs and went to school and volunteered for soup kitchens. The residents of Party Town thought, *Nasty!* Those things didn't sound fun. *Have a good time!* was their motto. Life was too short to be monkeying around with shit like that. Sure, sometimes people in Party Town got sick or died, but that was no reason not to keep partying. If you couldn't make lemonade out of lemons, you might as well be a tadpole or something. They were put here on Earth to live, dammit, and they were going to live. Funerals were even bigger parties than everyday parties because they wanted to show God or whoever was up there that *Hey, you aren't going to stop our fun, asshead!*

Nobody was sure, or could remember, where their food came from, or why they had power in their homes and gasoline in their cars, or whom to thank for the endless supply of wine, beer, and spirits. Whenever the topic came up, they would shrug and say, *Who the hell cares?* The less they thought about stuff like this, the better.

As the decades passed, the partying took a toll. Children, teens, and adults—they were all pretty haggard. Most were addicted to alcohol and cigarettes, and in some cases, narcotics. Men's bellies bloated; women's, too. Bad skin all around. Flabby, weak, and foggy-minded people. Lots of STDs: you name it, they had it. Fistfights, dramatic screaming matches. Lack of sleep and poor diet meant long-term issues like hepatitis and bone degeneration. Life expectancy kept shrinking, babies born with fetal alcohol syndrome, whatever. The people didn't get sad about this stuff. It was just the way it was. Whenever a person pointed out the problems in Party Town, another would be there to say, *There's always been problems, throughout history! We just like to* think *we have it worse now. It's so egotistical.*

Then they would hug tearfully and say, *Wow, remember how we always heard that life is short? Well it really is, man. It really is.* And they'd raise their glasses and toast. And they'd party even harder, in daylight and darkness.

The Kids in West End

The kids in West End make skid marks with their bicycles in the shapes of dogfish and parsley.

At night they float out of their bedroom windows. They hover above the dam, watching for spawning salmon, wondering if and when.

The kids in West End are on fire. At school they sizzle in their seats, triggering alarms, compromising test results. Their charred skin peels away, revealing a settlement much like an early American colony.

The kids in West End were born in a stand of trees near the highway. They burst out of their mothers like cannonballs and punched holes in a silo with their fleshy newborn selves.

Each day the kids in West End swap heads with one another. Nobody knows whose is whose. The gym teacher tells them apart by their elbows.

They tell fortunes by reading the cancer cells in their mothers' breasts.

One thousand times an hour they are distracted by chewing gum.

They must wipe their feet before coming into the kitchen, to erase the dissatisfaction from their soles.

They climb inside tractor tires and roll down the highway, ushered by breezes all the way to the ocean. In summer months they mimic cicadas and curse eternal life.

The kids in West End have been flagged for removal. They'll thank you for this later.

They are touching you in tender ways. One day they will open a book about long times coming. They'll know the ending even before it's read.

Blackout

She liked the way her feet sank into the wet sand as we walked. She said it felt like standing on the inside of a baked potato. Strolling along the coast of Phuket in early September was not ordinary, but I was tired of the poetic language she kept injecting into conversation. I disliked the metaphor. Her phrasing was forced. I pretended to contemplate the foamy water as it climbed the shore. She could step on all the metaphorical potatoes she wanted.

I prefer to say things without embellishment: The horizon was a pink and gold spill that neither of us wanted to clean. A breeze from across the ocean pushed Theresa's hair into her eyes.

Blackout

Thais and foreigners migrated from the road to watch the sunset. Lovers held hands. A Thai boy no older than ten sprinted along the shore. He waved a skewered hunk of pineapple over his head. On the wet beach where a finger of water crept up the sand, a blonde girl with her hair in cornrows lay on her belly and rested her chin on her palms. Her boyfriend leaned in and snapped the shutter of his camera.

I wondered where that photograph would end up and whether anyone would look at it in ten years and what they would think of it in that future.

Once the sun was gone, Theresa and I shook out our towels and headed to the road. I swatted sand from my feet and put on sandals, holding Theresa's shoulder for balance. Her feet were naked. We walked in the direction of our hotel. The broken sidewalks exposed the sewage lines. Even with dusk, the pavement must have been hot, and I marveled that Theresa would scald her soles just to feel like a native. Between buildings, dogs with hairless, distended bellies glanced up from their paws. They licked their snouts because they were too weak to lick us. We were making progress toward the hotel when Theresa stopped at a roadside vendor to buy a pineapple ice thing in a paper cup.

"You shouldn't eat that," I said. "They use tap water. They drag blocks of it down the street before they bust it up."

She chewed her purchase. "Want some?" she said. Her teeth were yellow. She gave the vendor an exorbitant tip, and he flashed his own yellow teeth.

I collapsed on the bed when we got to our hotel. I told Theresa to turn on the air conditioning. For twelve dollars we'd splurged and gotten a decent room above a restaurant. We even had English-speaking HBO. It was a clean room with a clean, tiled floor. Above our bed a black velvet painting of a tiger crouching among electric-pink jungle flora reminded us what country we were in.

Theresa took a shower, "to wash the sand from my body." I imagined her exposed bare skin being pummeled by the water, thousands of soothing assaults. I grabbed a Singha from the plastic bag. I snapped it open. Eight hours in the sun had left me tired and restless. The beer tasted good, and I wanted a cigarette.

From the balcony I could view the narrow street. Two bars sat on the corner. Open-air restaurants lined the block. The rumble of mopeds and trucks sounded from the main road, the persistent calls of "Sir! Sir! Transport?" and the crackling hum of an injured telephone pole.

I spotted prostitutes in every bar, among the Caucasians. The hookers approached the men; they talked, touched, accepted drinks. I wanted to hear the conversations, but the air conditioner was too noisy. I singled out a Thai girl with long hair, thin arms, and a mouth that hung open due to her large teeth. She sipped pink liquid through a straw. She was waiting for her future to approach and say, "Is this seat taken?"

I took a shower after Theresa. The tiles were gritty, and the hard water washed the salt from my skin. I came out of the bathroom carrying the towel. Outside, it was dark. For an hour, Theresa and I lay on the bed, drinking beer, watching TV. We started kissing, and before long I climbed on top of her. We hadn't had as much sex on this trip as we'd thought we would, so it seemed good and natural. My body was cool and clean as the air streamed over my back.

Then the power died. The lights went out—the television and air conditioner, too. John Denver's voice from a corner bar went silent. A collective gasp rose from the street. We continued our lovemaking, inspired by the serendipity of it all, but then Theresa started talking about how weird it was. I told her *shhhhhh*, a noise I'd wanted to make toward her for three months now. She took my suggestion and began gyrating. Puffing and moaning and all that stuff. I knew she was acting, but it didn't matter. We came together to the cheers of the crowd outside.

I smoked a cigarette on the balcony, noticing that the restaurants had distributed candles, which must have been why people cheered. Even with the candles, no one was talking much. The silence on the street was strange and heavy and overbearing. The only noises were crackles and pops of the power lines. It sounded like bacon frying.

Theresa was reading her book by flashlight. I had almost finished my cigarette when I heard her scream. I went in.

"There's a bat in here," she said. She had barricaded herself behind the two pillows in a corner of the bed.

I covered my head with my hands. I squatted forcefully and could feel the soft pack of cigarettes fold in my pocket.

"Where?" I said. I hated bats.

She poked the flashlight out of her sanctum and directed its beam toward a spot above the TV. I saw a brown lump on the ceiling. It didn't look big. I approached it with backpack held in front of my face and flashlight brandished like a club. As I was about to pounce, the bat launched.

It flapped chaotically around the room. Theresa screamed as I ducked and covered. I imagined all of the unpronounceable diseases this bat wanted to give us.

Our flashlight beams crossed each other as we tried to keep tabs on the creature. I told Theresa I was going to kill it. It rose and dipped and swooped around the room. I swung my backpack. Theresa insisted I shouldn't kill it. I asked her what she wanted to do. Instead of answering, she crawled forward and flung open the door to the hallway, but the bat kept terrorizing us from above.

"It's not going to just *leave*," I said. I was getting frustrated. The room was heating up, making it tough to breathe.

The bat landed on the wall above the bathroom door. I threw things, hoping to knock it down. "If I can stun it," I said, "we can chuck it out the window, and it'll survive."

I tossed Theresa's shoes and passport, my stick of deodorant, all the Baht change in my hip sack. Theresa started crying, because each failed attack was a step toward death. I lobbed everything in my reach smaller than a hiking boot, but the bat was untouchable. Theresa didn't want the bat to die. I told her to get help, and she stopped talking.

The bat launched into the air again, flapping in its delicate, drunken way. It lighted on the wall across the room, at hip-level. A high-pitched chirp, like a super-cricket, emanated from it, as shrill as an alarm clock. I thought for sure the natives on the street would rush up the steps to our room, summoned by its battle cry, to protect their indigenous friend.

"Why don't they get the fucking power on?" I whispered. I crept up to the bat and, in a sudden lunge, pinned it against the wall with my backpack. It squealed horribly.

My hope had been to squash the thing quick and pretty—I'd heard that bats were fragile—but instead, it had squeezed half of its body into a crack in the corner where the walls met. I had pinned its right wing. Its cries became painful to hear because of the volume, but more because I knew that this animal was simply screaming for its life.

I didn't see any choice. Theresa wanted me to coax the bat into the plastic bag that had held our beer—that was her word, "coax"—but there was no way I was letting that thing loose again. I stuck the flashlight in my mouth, leaned against the backpack with my shoulder, unzipped the front pocket, and drew out a sharpened pencil. While still applying pressure, I slid the backpack down the wall slowly, until I could see the bat. Its wing was huge. The flesh of its abdomen was soft, trembling, and covered with a thin layer of downy hair. Then its face appeared, poking out of the crack, looking like a newborn human infant; its eyes were squinted and its mouth was wide, emitting its plaintive cries.

I stabbed the pencil through its face. I pinned its head to the wall. Its chirping wound down slowly, like an electronic piano that had been unplugged.

Once it was dead, it shriveled up on the end of my pencil until it was barely bigger than a golf ball. Theresa's sobbing reminded me that I wasn't alone. I stuffed the strange little corpse into the bag, tied the bag shut, and dropped it in the bathroom garbage can.

I slept uncomfortably for half the night, tossing and turning in the heat. At some point, the power returned, surging to life and waking me. I climbed out of bed and killed the TV and the lights. Out on the street, the revelers roared; John Denver returned with a fury. The image of the bat's impaled face remained in my mind. Theresa wouldn't let me touch her, even after our sweat had dried and the air conditioning chilled our bodies.

★

The next morning, we ate in the restaurant below our room. I felt ambivalent about the breakfast, about the rest of our trip, about what would happen when we got back to Michigan. We had arranged for a minivan to take us to the

Phuket airport. We would fly to Hat Yai, a small city on the mainland, where we would stay one night before riding a bus into Malaysia. We'd been in Thailand for three weeks, in Southeast Asia for three months, living out of backpacks. To everyone we met, I was a customer, a big fat dollar sign. Or worse: If they knew I was American, I was a bully or a cowboy. They were partly correct. In the States, I wasn't much above the poverty line, but here, I was a king.

I didn't blame Theresa for this—not outright—but she did, after all, linger at merchant's tables. She actually *looked* at every sarong, handmade necklace, and knockoff gold watch they dangled in front of her eyes. She paid the women on the beach to twist her hair into cornrows and give her a massage. She sprinkled Bahts in front of the toothless men squatting in stairwells as if her money were fairy dust.

In the minivan, we were forced to sit in the back, crammed into a seat with no leg room. The driver stopped at other hotels and picked up four more passengers. Luggage piled around us until we were pinned in on both sides. In the town of Patong, the driver parked in an unpaved lot. He cut the engine. We waited. We waited, getting hotter. I looked at my watch; it was forty-five minutes before our flight. The driver dangled his arm out the window. He stuck a toothpick in his mouth. We waited. Even though Theresa's bare leg was pressed against mine, it was like we weren't touching. She had hardly said a word in the minivan; her poetic language was now just poetic breathing. We had argued about the bat during breakfast, with her saying that I shouldn't have killed it and me saying that I remembered her crying and not offering any suggestions. Over the heads of the other passengers, I asked the driver why we were sitting here. He said, "Minute. Another passenger, just minute." The driver wore mirrored sunglasses and kept pulling the toothpick out of his mouth to look at it like it was a thermometer.

I tried to read. Theresa hummed, which prevented me from reading. At last, the new passenger arrived. His head was wrapped in a white turban. He climbed into the van and threw his duffel bag onto the stack that had already blocked me in. He was old, brown-skinned, with a full, white beard, wearing heavy, black-rimmed glasses, carrying a briefcase. He sat in front of me; I imagined the bomb in his briefcase.

The van sped away. We raced over hills, over the countryside. The driver must have sensed that we were all doomed: He took terrible risks; he hit curves at horrific speeds, straddling the center line. I made an effort to catalogue the distant jagged mountains, the glistening rice paddies, the water buffaloes poised like statues in the stands of palm trees. The driver wanted to kill us, or at least to make us think about death.

I did think about death, as I often had, but this time it was a refusal to die beside a woman I would never love, a woman who would later miscarry my child, a woman who would cause me to break eleven bones in my hand. I refused to die in a country where nobody knew my side of the story.

We soared at ninety miles an hour. I recalled the Ray Bradbury tale about a man who travels back in time to the age of the dinosaurs and, even though he tries not to, changes the future because he accidentally steps on a butterfly. This man started in the present; he went back to the past and messed with things; when he returned to the present, he could easily identify the damage he'd caused.

I looked out the window at the blurred landscape. I looked at the other people in the van—the terrorist, the driver's mirrored eyes, Theresa. Nobody was sharing my experience.

But still, I tried. I'm sure of it. I searched everywhere for signs.

~~I Killed~~ the Invisible Man

BOXED?
KO'D?
OR ...

IF THE INVISIBLE MAN DIES AND
NOBODY SEES IT, DOES HE REALLY
DIE?

opening 1

~~It's~~ one of the ironicalities of the entertainment-based country we live in that the truth is overshadowed by the fake fiction. The craziest characters that explode from the brains of their creators become more memorable and "real" than their true-life counterparts. It probably all boils down to originality.

* * *

opening 2

~~Us Americans love an original. What I'm saying is that if we wake up tomorrow to find gorillas screaming at us about the hole in the ozone, we won't be surprised. That's how powerful *Planet of the Apes* is in our minds. "Damn you all to Hell!"~~

* * *

opening 3

Roy Green was a plain old Midwesterner. Lanky, six-four, 162 pounds, gray by forty-one. Not a good-looking dude, and buttery skin because of how much Kentucky bourbon he drank. He was an amazing referee but not swift. A guy who changed physics and the laws of the universe without even trying...and still a lousy boxer!

Another problem is = hardly anyone believes Roy even existed. Which maybe he didn't. Which is what makes him a giant fucking deal. (crap, but keep for now)

* * *

opening 4

~~Everyone knows a "Roy Green," or someone with a name just as easy and American. Like Carl Folds. Dennis Mock. Paul Garner. No one would suspect a dude with such a dopey basic name to be outstanding. Rocky Balboa. Mohammad Ali. Leon Sphinx. These are names of greatness. Roy Green? His name's important not only because what happened to him could happen to any of us, but even more frightening is the symbolism.~~ (What was I talking about here?)

* * *

opening 5   BEST ONE - KEEP IT SIMPLE, STUPID!!!

Roy Green was a very tall, very gifted man. He had a wife named Bridgett and a daughter named Pearl. He had a high talent for refereeing boxing matches, which was his job until the Eastern Michigan Golden Gloves Commission wouldn't let him do it anymore.

His job was also loving his family, and he got paid in hugs and kisses more valuable than all the gold bullion in the Egyptian kingdom. Roy got so much power from his "ladies," as he called them. I myself witnessed how happy they made the guy.

TOO MUCH B.S.?

If the Invisible Man Dies and Nobody Sees It, Does He Really Die?

He was 42, Bridgett was 30, and Pearl was just 13 when Roy woke up one Saturday and wasn't there anymore.

No one could see him. He couldn't see himself. Presto! Like a magician's rabbit, except he could talk and scream and touch things, whereas the rabbit is gone totally. Which of these would be a worse fate? Read on and find out...

THAT I AM GATHERING.? SHOULD I NAME HER.?

According to actual testimony Roy lost his mind for a few hours that day, as in it literally jumped out of his head and ran to the Stop-N-Go for a pack of Kools. He collapsed on the bathroom floor, all spasms and puke...and yes, his puke was invisible. And NO, don't feel gross for asking!

When Bridgett finally got home and went to take a shower and happened to "find" Roy and run her fingers along his body (this mental picture is gross, lol) after first freaking out over hearing the cabinets being thumped but seeing no one doing the thumping she fainted right on top of her invisible husband and his barf. She must've looked goddamn ~~stupid~~ *crazy* just laying there six inches off the ground. It actually makes me laugh thinking about it.

(CUT IT? SOUNDS COLD BUT RUINS TRANSITION IF I DO.)

GENTLE

Except this isn't a funny story, at all. Roy Green never hurt anyone. He was a ~~wimpy~~ referee who cared about his beautiful, proud fighters and the art of the canvas. He wasn't sitting on a mountain of cash, couldn't buy diamond bracelets for his daughter. ~~He couldn't even fix her tee~~th ~~because he spent half his money on bets~~. That's probably why he named her Pearl, because she was ~~the only jewel he needed or~~ the only jewel he could afford. (MAYBE THIS IS MY TITLE) He lived in a house the color of a grocery bag with flaking siding and a 9x7 rectangle of grass out front. New siding was WAY out of the budget of such a simple referee so the rust stains kept growing like The Blob. He stuck to ref'ing because he had no other skills unless you count criticizing his wife's fingernails and ass. Plus, he loved to be in the middle of all the sweat and fists of fury that is my craft.

That's right...I am one of his fighters. Derrick the Terrible. Fifty wins, eleven by knockout, only one loss, and many fair fights thanks to Roy Green.

(TAKE OUT ME HERE — NOT WHAT THIS STORY IS ABOUT!)

* * *

Bridgett and Pearl figured out pretty soon that the man they loved was just a nothing. ~~Like I'd been saying for months except now it was true like science fiction.~~

He was the real invisible man. THIS IS NOT A TEST.

His body vanished and his clothes, too, because whatever he was wearing when he disappeared also disappeared. Actually don't quote me on this. He might have slept in the raw. I never asked even if I did love the man. However, I know for sure that the clothes Roy put on after he was invisible DID NOT turn invisible. Which is why he didn't wear clothes anymore.

Bridgett tried to hide Roy's invisible quality from the world, which sounds cracked, trying to hide something you can't see. So I guess technically she tried to unhide him, but he refused to be unhidden. He wouldn't wear clothes. But she was a convincing lady and she wrapped his face and hands with the same tape us boxers use on our fists. It made him look like the real invisible man you've seen in those films. I personally like the Chevy Chase one. Roy died twenty years ago now, and you wouldn't believe how many invisible man movies they've made in twenty

7 - DO I LIST THEM? *Doyle*

years even though none are based on Roy, big surprise. That will all change when people read my story...

* * *

The year was 1983. A year of cool dancing and good coke. Every fighter did it so don't blame me. Anyway, the past's the past, and I was a dumbass with a pretty face and tight bod fresh out of high school. No one ever sets out to get hooked on the white stuff and same with me I didn't. But any addict'll tell you once it happens you'll do anything to get it, even stealing from someone you love or destroying your career with violence.

(EXPAND THIS PART? ADD "YOUNG, DUMB AND FULL OF CUM" LINE.)

Kids ALWAYS think that being invisible would be the coolest. Ten out of ten it's the second choice when you ask what super power they want. Usually right after flying. But flying would be great, whereas invisibility is awesome in fantasy but horse shit in reality. Thank God for Bridgett and Pearl, the two women who saved Roy's life. Well, they didn't actually save it. He died. But they let him live while he was alive. Kids think, "Wow I can spy on girls in the shower and make the teacher fall down the stairs. I'll be a hero." Roy

TITLE - HE LIVED WHILE HE WAS ALIVE?

never wanted to do anything like that with his invisible powers. Maybe he should have...

Roy only ~~pretended t~~o TRIED TO get on with his life. After he stopped crying that he couldn't see himself, he collected Bridgett and Pearl to discuss what was what. He was set on NO DOCTORS at least not right away. He thought maybe his body would reappear naturally with more vegetables or a better mattress. He was a nasty insomniac most of his life. The irony is that the day he woke up invisible he'd had the best sleep he could remember! That's what he told me anyway. ~~Bridgett hadn't come home that night, which Mr. Fifth of J&B hadn't even noticed, so I guess the sleep thing he said is probably true.~~

Bridgett said she would go to a farmer's market (yeah right) for corn and peaches and learn how to make those protein shakes that keep us boxers trim and nice-looking. Chances are her hands were shaking when she said this. She was still upset bu~~t not so much by the invisibility~~ I ~~don't thin~~k and couldn't look at Roy, even though Roy was an empty recliner so really Bridgett was looking at him no matter where she was looking if you think about it.

MENTION THAT THIS WAS ROY'S FAVORITE CHAIR AND THE SPOT WHERE IT HAPPENED.

Surprisingly Pearl wasn't freaked out by her dad's invisibleness. ~~Teenagers are fucking crazy, but they're probably the wisest citizens on Earth.~~ She thought it was wicked and whacked and she couldn't wait to invite her friends over, but Bridgett was as white as a new Microsoft Word page, so Pearl promised not to tell anyone. She was skinny and shy and listened to heavy metal rock. ~~She dressed in short shorts and was beginning to blossom into a beauty and she~~ was also ~~sweet and never swore, which is~~ amazing ~~considering the shitmouths her daddy and mommy were.~~

* * * *SOUNDS LIKE A CHILD—
CHECK IF B.M. MEANS THE SAME THING.*

Let's get the basics out of the way. His doo-doo was invisible. This was true for every bodily fluid—snot, pee, blood, tears. Roy made these things and they stunk and were felt, (mention when he spit on me?) but they sure didn't show up in a photograph or a mirror. Not there, but there. Get it? Fingerprints DID show up, though. Cops dusted the scene and found Roy's prints, but the question is—Were they from before or after he turned invisible? My opinion was WHO CARES? The dude is dead. Let him lie.

Roy ate the same as when he was visible except LOTS MORE. Fries, hamburgers, Cokes, donuts. It was like he thought eating would make him reappear again. He started with healthy food but Bridgett didn't know shit about lo-fat cooking, and after two weeks of invisibleness Roy pigged out on whatever his ladies bought him.

And yes the eating was freaky. Picture it. A hot dog in a bun, smothered in kraut and ketchup. Now the hot dog floats off the table, hangs in mid-air. WHAT?? Then a chunk rips loose and gets mangled and mashed and pulverized before your eyes. I felt like I was on some Superman acid ~~which truthfully I might've been~~. Then right as the mush starts going down and you think it's going to splat on the chair, the mush vanishes. (dissolves?) Talk about questioning God!

This is from an eyewitness perspective. I don't mind telling you I was the first and only boxer to see Roy in his condition. There I go again, saying see when all I saw was the recliner with a groove in the cushion. Roy's butt was making that groove. He was naked and looking at me. Son of a bitch, it felt weird! His voice boomed and I left my skin in a pile on the floor when I jumped. Pearl laughed so hard she fell down next to it. Bridgett cracked up, too. I wanted to call the mental hospital right there. ~~Not for the ladies, but for me because I could hear Roy laughing and I wanted to bust his fucking skull open like a beer can.~~

* * *

I need to back up and get to the story.

OR MAYBE THE REAL STORY IS NOW?

So Roy hasn't been around the Saginaw Boxing Club for three weeks. He's missed the last four fights he should've ref'd. The trainers and fighters are saying he's got cancer or Bridgett cheated on him and he's so depressed he can't get out of bed. Then out of nowhere BAM, a phone call. Remember this is 1983, before cells. Everyone can hear the ringing through the loudspeakers, louder than the boom box. Willie Vargas the gym manager yells at me that some chick's on the line. I stop my bag routine and go answer it. I'm high and thinking *This better be Bridgett, because you were supposed to leave him three weeks ago and why haven't you called me?*

"D the T here."

"Don't talk. Listen." He was shit-faced. "Bridgett is on her way." I found out later he'd made Pearl ask for me, and she was who the "chick" was.

He was so drunk I couldn't recognize his voice. I said, "Roy?"

"Say my name again and I bounce your balls on the sidewalk. I told you not to speak. Don't tell anybody about this call. Be out front in twenty-five."

"I got the Osthwello fight in two weeks, Roy."

"SHUT UP YOU MISERABLE PRICK SHUT UP!!"

How can I write it so it sounds like it did? More exclamation points? Or a font like 72?

Twenty minutes later I'm freezing my ass off. It's January and the snow is a foot high. For you California people this isn't any Little House on the Prairie frosting. This is downtown Saginaw snow, crusty and black in the gutter, gray Slurpee on the sidewalks. Same color as my toenails. I didn't mind. My life WAS these streets. Ash and Hermansau is where I first popped a tooth out of a guy's head. My uppercut sent him to the cement, and I was fourteen. Got a reputation as a slugger who could take punishment after two spics jumped me outside Kentucky Fried Chicken where I worked to help my mom pay rent. The spics hit me with a sawed-off cue until they thought I was out. While they were trying to lift my wallet I swatted the long-hair in the nuts and broke the fat guy's mouth. By the time I was seventeen, I hit the ring. I could take anything these fuckers dished, and I wanted to beat my way to a title someday. And if that didn't work out, I wanted to teach kids how to punch and be disciplined and become men in their lives.

But I'll say it, Roy scared me on the phone. He sounded mad as an animal. I figured B had told him and he was going to do a driveby. I prayed an Our Father and smoked a cigarette. My life was just beginning, even though I didn't know it at the time.

Bridgett drove up in the car. If there was any justice in the world, people would know what a classic beauty [JORMAL: PERSON.] this lady was. I guess that's my job. She wasn't trashy like you see nowadays ringside with the low-cut blouses, big fake boobs [BREASTS] and jewels. Matter of fact, B didn't care for boxing except that it gave Roy a paycheck. The other fighters called her "Ice Princess," which was bullshit seeing how us guys were supposed to be like ice and pound each other's faces, so why shouldn't a woman? I guess I was a fighter for women's rights as well as a fighter for glory.

Still, she *did* act like a bitch that day. I got in her Plymouth and she didn't even see me. I was just another ring-jock that her husband spent time with. If anyone looked could they tell she was in love with me? (*WAS* she, asshole? Pearl says NO, stupid.)

I asked her what the hell's going on and are you still with him? I'd rode my bike past their house ninety times in three weeks so I already knew the answer to my questions, which is what any good lawyer will do.

She said, "Don't start," and pushed me off when I tried to kiss her.

I said, "You disappear for two weeks and now it's don't start?" Three months we'd been sneaking around and I was thinking it was finally going to be in the open and I would move in with the woman of my dreams while Roy wound up sipping rainwater off trash bags. But while we drove I smelled something rotten in that car.

"Things got more complicated, sweetheart. Put it that way."

Sometimes she talked to me like I was a baby which was whatever, what did I care as long as other people didn't hear it. Actually, my mom

~~talked to me that way. What can I say, women want to baby me. Must be this pretty face~~. I cracked the dash with a punch and imagined it was Roy. ~~Then I remembered it was Bridgett's car and I'd have to pay for the crack, and I star~~ted ~~crying.~~ I busted out the vial and sniffed a couple before I saw where we were heading...**west on State Street**?! My eyes popped out of my face.

It was her and Roy's house!

* * *

Now get this clear. I'm a traditional dude. ~~My folks would have been married forever if my dad hadn't found a better wife~~. Yes I did the hardcore drug scene, walked the walk of the streets, but deep down, I'm clean with Christian values. I go to bed wearing gold crosses every night, and you can ask my wife. That's what nobody understands when I tell them what happened.

INTRODUCED Bridgett dragged me to their house and ~~showed~~ me to the Invisible Man ~~just like I already wrote back on page seve~~n. I flipped out for a while and had to run down to the bar for some shots, which I could hardly swallow I was shaking so bad. Eventually I got steady and came back ready to face thi~~s freaky asshole~~. I'd fought plenty of guys more dangerous than Roy and what did I

If the Invisible Man Dies and Nobody Sees It, Does He Really Die?

care if I couldn't see him, I'd still harm his face. Not that I was thinking about doing it! I was a professional amateur fighter, but I mean to say that out of self-defense I would have murdered him if it came to that.

Turns out I didn't have to. Bridgett confessed to the hotels and secret phone calls, even the ~~no-lube buttfucking and~~ other sexual experiments. I admit I got scared. She reveals all this in Roy's dinky living room, and all I can do is stare at the groove in the Lay-z Boy that tells me HE's really sitting there and isn't sneaking up to slit my throat. When Bridgett brought up the ~~anal detail~~, STUFF I almost chugged out the door, but Roy's voice came out of nowhere asking for a bourbon. I jumped up and got it. Watching the glass in mid-air wasn't easy but it beat the hell out of not knowing where he was!

(TAKING TOO LONG — GET TO THE JIST)

Roy drank some bourbon and then said this statement that almost made me puke: "I would like it if you kept screwing my wife." Those were the words I heard out of nowhere!

Turns out that's how Bridgett had described our "love." Three months of screwing. No emotion. I didn't have time to get pissed. I was trying to digest this new surprise...the Invisible Man giving me thumbs up? He talked more in his weird unseen voice. I could keep doing his wife in his house, in his bed. He was blasted, but Roy had been blasted for years so I knew he did not joke.

I know what you're thinking. Sweet deal. A nineteen-year-old dude banging a mature lady with her husband's approval? Sounds cooler than real life! TITLE- COOLER THAN REAL LIFE?

Truth is, real life was never cool for me. My dad worked night security at the sewage treatment plant until I was 10, meaning I never hung out with him. My mom did hair every night. They weren't bad parents, but they had debt from hospital bills when my mom had cancer. With no siblings I was a latchkey squirt with nowhere to play and no one to talk to. When my dad fell for a cocktease I started shadowboxing. I couldn't read because of dyslexia, so it's a Hollywood fairytale that here I am at forty years young writing a book, selling real estate, and finishing my Associates at Saginaw Community. ~~Now THAT's an American original!~~

I took up fighting when I was Pearl's age and put my heart, guts, and balls into it. Sure, money and ladies were part of the plan that never came to be, but mostly the ring was where I felt like a battleship and I wanted to lead by example. **Derrick the Terrible, Eastern Michigan Golden Gloves Featherweight Champion 1981 and 1982.** I lit up so many guys, it feels spectacular to land a hook to the top of his nose and watch a fighter drop like the power button's been clicked off. When a kid's got no bank account, no education, no skills, no dad...this makes him a king.

I wasn't King Derrick at the Roy Green house, though. Bridgett made me ride my Huffy over after my workout, two miles one way. She cooked dinner for Roy, Pearl, and me ~~even though she wasn't much of a cook~~. I stole tape from the gym so Pearl could somewhat wrap her dad, I mean two half-assed strips across his nose and forehead and that's about all. He didn't want anything near his mouth, eyes, neck, ears, or hair. His wrists got covered to the palms but not around the fingers, so you saw basically three sections of floating white tape that had nothing to do with each other and you couldn't make it look like a person even if you tried and it sucked. ~~And Roy sucked, too.~~ He wanted to be invisible, and when no one was wat*c*hing [GODDAMN IT] he would yank off the tape. He spent days and days in the raw. I saw what a drunken mess he was. STOP USING THE WORD SAW!!!

Roy gobbled whatever B stuck in front of him. At dinners this is what I encountered. Pearl served him bourbon or PBR in a glass. She smiled at me sometimes, which wow, I thought, what a trooper. Six drinks a sitting that guy drank, I shit you not. Also, I don't know if it was the invisibleness, or Bridgett's cooking, or Roy's normal routine, but he passed gas. Wet, crackly gas. I lost my appetite while B and P forked potatoes like everything was hunky dory. Then the sicko would start ranting how fighters used to be real men and "not the delinquent spics with spaghetti arms we got now." I'm no spic, but lots of my buddies were, and this racism pissed me off, but I kept my mouth closed and sipped my Pabst. I mean did I have a choice?

Night after night, Roy farted and talked garbage about Saginaw gloves like I wasn't five feet away. Then me and Bridgett headed upstairs while Pearl washed dishes. Invisible Roy sat in his kitchen chair and swatted flies. At least he <u>said</u> he was swatting flies. When we walked out of the room he always said, "You two have fun. I'll be here killing these flies," and like magic the broom closet opens and the swatter floats out, and we see his chair sliding up to the table.

The kitchen was situated right under the marriage bedroom, so while me and Bridgett had sex we could hear WHAP, WHAP, WHAP... "Son of a bitch, that one's trying to fight me..." WHAP, WHAP, WHAP...

When I complained, Bridgett told me to shut up and kiss her. She said at least we knew where he was. She said would I like it better if he was sitting by the bed while we did it, because how would we even know?

I'm a good Christian boy so I never believed something so perverted was possible, but after Bridgett's comment I couldn't stop thinking about it. I checked over my shoulder while I went at her a~~nd sometimes this made it tough to get it~~ up. I knew that if we could hear the flyswatter then Roy and Pearl could hear us. Add in my coke addiction and you've got a humongous situation brewing, and weird sex drives.

This went on for ten days. Me coming over, dinner, me and Bridgett moving upstairs for drugs and action. At 11:00 p.m. I'd ride back to my apartment hopefully without ~~seeing~~ GODDAMN IT! RUNNING INTO Roy on my way out.

It's not an ideal situation, right? But if Roy and B are fine with it, what do I care? At least we don't need to sneak around anymore. These were my thoughts way back when. Maybe Roy can't get it up? Remember this is years before Viagra, which would be a shame and who can blame a woman for getting some if this is the case? I told myself this must be the deal, which made it easier to take B in their marriage bed night after night.

Still though, even while we were hooking up constantly, B was distant. I tried to get her to admit she loved me, but she wouldn't with Roy in the house. So something had changed, right? Something besides Roy vanishing? I'm no idiot. I fought with B to get her to admit something big. That the day Roy turned invisible she was planning to leave him, but when she fainted in the bathroom she experienced a vision and changed her mind. She would "work things out" because he was an imperfect but not a bad man. He'd done the best he could for her and Pearl and didn't deserve to be on the street. I wanted her to come clean and admit this was the truth.

You're probably saying, "But where did you fit in, D the T?" Well believe you me I was asking that same question. Only I didn't ask it out loud, which I should have...

* * *

Then one night while we're getting down, I hear her scream, "Yes! Yes! Do me!" Except B has never screamed words like this, and it's not a woman's voice that's screaming, it's a man pretending to be a woman. And it's right next to my ear!

~~I about crapp~~ed. B giggled so hard she choked, and I heard Roy laughing, too. I leapt off the bed and threw jabs at the air with my junk flopping out of my boxers. I was seeing more red than an American Chinese flag. My junk made Roy laugh louder until I yanked the blanket from B and tossed it at the spot where I heard Roy. He knocked over a lamp trying to dodge, but the blanket covered him, and suddenly there was a person underneath it.

"Caught you, you perverted son of a bitch!" I yelled. I wrestled his bony ass to the floor like a fish. "You get your jollies watching me, old man?" It took all I had not to beat his face in. Really it was because I cared so much about B and saw how scared and annoyed she was that I let him live...that time.

(I need to go back and cut whenever I call him creep or drunk or anything that isn't "funny bad" like the gas, or else ask her to read it and see what

(she'll let me keep, because I don't know why I shouldn't tell the truth, I mean nobody's perfect and so what if the invisible man was a dick, nobody even knew this guy or knows who I am and who cares??????)

* * *

So imagine you're a dinner guest at the invisible man's house. After grub, you and the invisible man's wife ~~who you're in love wi~~th go up the creaky steps to the queen-sized bed while the invisible man kills flies and sings Billy Joel and his daughter washes the dishes. Night after night, instead of spooning, you ride your bike across town to your apartment, even though the invisible man is passed out in front of the news and wouldn't give two shits if you slept in his bed or not.

And sometimes on your way out, when you're walking down the stairs into the living room with the TV glow, you see Pearl on the loveseat under a blanket. She just watches you with her big white eyes. That's the last image you see when you go to sleep in your bed. That's the thing you start looking forward to during this whole deal.

I'm going to just say it. This eighth grader's eyes were goddamn sexy. Don't think I didn't feel like a creep. I ran out of there every night, biked through the rain, stopped at a bus stop for a snort and swore at my uncontrolled ass for even having these dirty thoughts. But still Pearl crept into my head. Those were low times. I had nosebleeds. I was sipping from the invisible man's bourbon, riding my bike wasted. I couldn't concentrate and lost control in general, such as when I knocked out Willie Vargas while we were sparring.

Because of the invisible man it was tough to make love to B, and besides, her attitude was different. Before the vanishing happened, she would stroke my chest and call me "beautiful creature." Now she was making fun of me and showed more cleavage. Then there was the constant wondering about the man who wasn't there, or maybe WAS! Add in the teenage daughter giving me erotic stares and I was a Hercules mess ready for rehab or to get arrested for statutory rape.

Banging a mom while her husband watched, getting nasty looks from her daughter? It sounds like porno fantasy #1. But in my own words, "it made me sick." And I'll just write it now so I can be off the hook—I married that daughter! That's right, I took Pearl down the aisle four years later, so it all worked out.

CAN I POSSIBLY KEEP THIS?

* * *

First though, there was trouble. Pearl ran away.

Would it hurt my story to tell how I killed him? How I wasn't even pissed about how B made me feel or about Pearl coming on to me, or wasn't weirded out, truthfully. I was angry in general, plain and simple. Moldy anger that grows in a guy's stomach and rolls against his ribs. The truth? Roy hurt me like an ax. He had been like a dad, I felt that way about him. With my dad being gone to Florida with a woman I won't even call a lady, what's a guy to do? My mother took care of me and I loved her, but she couldn't give me the same concepts about me a man could.

What does it feel like to kill an invisible man? I don't know. I mean, I do know, but how can I really KNOW if I didn't see it?

I don't see his face. I do see a face but not his. All I remember is that that fucker had some fight in him, Wild Turkey or no.

This is the '80s I might remind you before any CSI DNA FBI magic, and it's a good thing because he popped my nose and I bled all over that carpet. I know *I* was there.

What there wasn't was Roy. He was no longer. No body, no nothing. ~~And the truth is he WASN'T these things even before I massacred him using the same skills he ad~~ored.

(not sure where the plot is going if I can't say what happened (check with her) what can I say other than how I went looking for Pearl when she ran away because Roy didn't care and neither did B, they were rotten parents and showed their true colors and what happened probably would have happened no matter what)

* * *

Pearl vanished with only her clothes and a bunch of Roy and B's cash. Bridgett said, "She's a big girl, she can take care of herself," and pestered me about money like I had something to do with Pearl running off. Not that B wanted to get back at me because it had been true, which it wasn't, just that it was a solid fact in her mind. I'd driven her daughter away, period. But I didn't put much stock in B's mouth those days. She had shadows from no sleep and there was a gray haze in her eyes I'd never seen. I was doing a lot of drugs at the time and I remember thinking about Bridgett: "Her eyes are Magic Markers."

She didn't see me when she spoke. Her eyes saw the wall or once in a while my stomach, and she licked her lips and said, "I'm more afraid for us than for Pearl. She's in Reno with a false ID, guarantee, losing our money at the crap table."

Long and short of it, B said they were out of cash thanks to Pearl and I was supposed to help. Invisible Roy couldn't exactly ref a fight, remember.

Roy tortured me to make me do it. Worse than lurking next to my ~~bare-ass~~ UNCLOTHED while I made love to his wife torture is what I mean. Assorted torture. He snorted lines from under my nose. Tripped me on my way to the bathroom. Stuck his tongue in my ear. A fucking nightmare of invisibility.

Why didn't you just leave, D the T? is what you're asking. Keep it Simple, Stupid. If you look closely, the answer is always the stupid one. Cocaine, crack, weed, booze. We were all three of us separated from the world for a string of days I can't see in my mind.

It all tested me. Every minute I was jumping out of my skin or cackling like a witch. Or the invisible man French inhaled a floating cigarette. Or I was facedown on the coffee table with my eyeballs pouring out. I had to fight back the violent urges from misery and glee, both.

What happens when something from your dreams actually happens? You go fucking insane. That's a super power no one wants.

My super power is living and surviving. You can ask Pearl how I put myself through college even when my brain has been diagnosed damaged. I boxed for four years after Roy died, had a decent record of either 12-4 or 5-9, I can't remember. Some days I feel jealous of Roy's invisible power, my face is so gross now and with the rejection looks I get from girls at the Big Apple Bagel. Well, not gross. Pearl says I'm a good-looking guy that looks like Lieutenant Dan from the Forrest Gump movie, but she's my wife. Her mom Bridgett is out of the picture. She went to rehab smartly and moved to Florida but passed away a couple years ago, which is why I can write this now.

Roy and B wanted me to throw a fight. The plan was for the Osthwello match, and we were going to use The Invisible Man to make me win. I don't remember the details.

So how did Bridgett explain her husband being gone? Because yes, some people asked about

Roy. Well, she said he was gone. Just that. Sad as it sounds, no one questions a guy splitting on his family.

> THE STORY IS OVER! JUST GET IT OUT!

* * *

FIXED

Okay, the fight never happened. Nothing was fixed at all. One night after dinner, I waited until I was drunk and pounced on that invisible prick right as he was cracking a joke about my crooked nose. Or maybe he wasn't saying anything, only sitting in the recliner with a floating glass of bourbon that I swatted away before I became Eye of the Tiger. Bam bam bam. I felt his teeth against my knuckles. I kept punching, thick dead noises under my fists. He wasn't screaming or begging, fucker was probably so soused he couldn't even feel it, but he did grunt. Or who knows, maybe he wanted to be punched? Maybe he baited me like a trout and I took the bait? I felt his blood on my fingers even though I couldn't see it, which was amazing. Here I am doing this raunchy damage and experiencing sensations of spit and spattering, but everything is clean—me, my two hands, the chair. No visual evidence except for gashes opening on my knuckles from where his teeth are cutting them. Then I feel a sledgehammer on my nose that is Roy's fist, and I can't see.

B pulled me off and slapped me a few times.

I wanted to tell the story of a heroic referee here but didn't do it well. I don't know what kind of story this is since it's not even a true one.

Here's the fact...I lied. Not about the invisible man or what I did to his face and wife, but that Pearl is with me. She's not here, and I didn't marry her. Who knows where she is. The truth is she ran away. Thirteen years old. Her mom doesn't even care much even though she cries now and then, but usually when she wants a favor.

Me and B stuck it out a few months and tried to make it work, but we were both so fucked up on substances that I left her. Roy's body disappeared. Or I mean it had already disappeared, but the disappeared body disappeared. Nobody couldn't even find that anymore. B filed a missing persons report, but they couldn't locate the disappeared body, so what me and B were left with was exactly nothing.

I'd like to say people missed Roy Green, but no one did. Not the fighters, not the refs, not the gym owners. B sort of missed him, and she ripped me a new one when I gave his clothes to the Salvation Army, but she and I were doomed like star-crossed individuals who sometimes resorted to pushing and insults. Four years later, Derrick the Terrible retired. It was the drugs and booze's fault, which is what B said before she went to rehab in Detroit. I moved to Cheboygan to live with my cousin and her boys. I started digging ditches for Consumers Energy. Fast forward twenty years and here I am with my realtor's license! In good shape for an older dude and almost out of college with a business degree. B found me after rehab, and she's been my wife now for nineteen years.

What I always hate is that we lost Pearl. In my dreams I pick Pearl up off that torn couch and run out the front door, and this means she never runs away, never steals B and Roy's money, and so Roy and B never ask me to take a dive, and so I never punch the hell out of Roy's face, and so nobody ever cries to me that he's dead and basically guilts me into marrying them.

Me and B live with two cats, who are Mickey and Balboa. Awesome animals. Pearl is 33 or 34 now, a woman. This is what I believe personally. She's out there and alive.

B doesn't talk about Pearl. She'd rather nag me to write this book. She's been doing it for years, telling me to take a class to learn writing and all that and that we'll be able to pay off our debts and get a new house if I can put my story on the page. She still won't say I love you. I don't need a word though, to know the truth. I try on this book but never get too far, probably because my heart's not in it. Also, it's impossible to concentrate with the headaches and the fucking haunted house we live in.

I hear footsteps but I don't see anyone. I hear the backdoor open and shut. I have three beers in the fridge only to go and find two or even one. Sometimes B looks like she's smirking, and I wonder: Is Roy still here? Was this their plan? Was it even their plan to lose their daughter?

I wonder how tough it would be for the invisible man to hide right under my nose all these years. Probably not at all. B's been handling the bills and money as long as I can remember since my brain can't concentrate for numbers. B does the shopping, B's home all day while I try to sell houses that nobody keeps buying.

Some nights I wake up to a whisper, "You could never punch." Or "Derrick the Turdburglar." Or "You think you could kill anything with those spaghetti arms?" Of course, no one's there. That doesn't stop me from answering ~~that prick~~, though. I tell him he's a freeloader and a disrespecter of the sport I love. I say, "You wanted me to cheat, but I have integrity. So keep eating my food and drinking my booze. I sleep with your wife every night and don't forget it." B rolls over and smacks me.

How long can it keep going? I guess it's been two decades so why stop now. I could save up and hop a plane and search the USA for Pearl, but that would be as crazy as wanting to be a champion. Almost nobody makes it, even ones with the gift. No thanks, I'll stick to my six weeks of spring every year and a warm bed.

~~I don't know if this will make a good movie but it WILL make a good one if anyone ever wants to try hard with it.~~

NEED A BETTER ENDING — MAKE SOMETHING UP?

Session 3

Q: What sort of life would it be if you could achieve everything you ever wanted?

A: You're talking basically about a piranha vs. tiger situation. Both are predators, but one hunts alone while the other hunts in a pack. Or really a school. Hunting is survival but it's also an art form, passed to each generation through genes and maybe through communication, definitely in the case of the tiger. Remember that neither of these beasts could tell you what a bongo is used for. Neither could describe a passage from an article about contaminated painkillers. And yet we're still scared of these animals. In a perfect world I could walk right up to a tiger crouching in the high grasses of India and slap his face and say, "Get lost, asshole. You and me, we don't get along." So yes, it would be a perfect life if I could do that. Just once I'd love to do that. My god. It'd be a hell of a lot better than sitting here with you.

Q: Please give a detailed description of your mind.

A: Let's say you're standing at a bus stop in the pouring rain, mostly protected by the shelter—you know, one of those plastic boxes with the bench inside?—but the rain is coming down so hard, and puddles are everywhere, and the roof is dripping and it's splashing your new loafers. These are really nice loafers that you paid good money for, and they're getting ruined. So when a person, let's say a middle-aged man who isn't remarkable except for his bushy mustache, which looks like something that went out of fashion in the 1940s, steps into the shelter, closes his umbrella, and turns to you and says, "Really coming down, huh?" Is it ethically irresponsible to ignore this man? Is this type of generic communication—meaningless, space-filling quote-unquote conversation, essential for society to function? Is this trivial exchange of pleasantries actually the fabric that keeps our human train chugging along? Forget love, forget scientific progress, forget painting, music, ballet, sketch comedy. Maybe none of that matters if a person doesn't feel this overwhelming urge to look at that mustachioed man and say, "Sure is."

Q: Tell me your dream.

A: I was in a massive toy store. Like with multiple floors that featured different types of toys on each floor. Escalators connecting the different levels. I went into the men's room and there were all these kittens in there. Dozens, maybe hundreds of tiny newborn kittens, and I had to watch where I stepped because I was terrified of squashing one under my foot. The bathroom was filthy, but I can't really describe precisely what made it filthy. Just a general feeling of grossness and grime, and the unsavory weirdness of all these kittens. Then suddenly a kid was in the bathroom with me, and he picked up one of the kittens and before I knew it the kitten was dead, with a part of its heart or brain protruding out of its head. It seemed that the kid had twisted the kitten or snapped it somehow, although that wouldn't explain why a red clumpy organ was emerging from it. In real life, this would have been a horrifying thing to witness, but in the dream I was OK with it because there were so many kittens. I guess it seemed unavoidable that some of them would die.

Session 3

After this bathroom scene, I was abruptly being pursued by—get this—one of the toys. This crazed dinosaur-like thing (that's the best I can describe it), made of rubber and as tall as a full-grown man. It walked on two legs and had a human face, featureless except for slit eyes and a mouthful of fleshy teeth. It wore a pre-made angry facial expression that never changed. Anyway, this creature was after me. Like, *after me*. This fucker wasn't going to stop until it caught me and killed me. It had a single purpose in life: my destruction. I was terrified and kept running to different levels of the store, searching for anything I could use as a weapon. Only now the toy store no longer had shelves with toys on them. Now each floor was unfinished, with scraps of lumber and old doors and junk like that, unpainted drywall and so on. I'm not sure why I couldn't just pick up a 2 x 4 or something of that nature to defend myself with, but I couldn't. With each moment I became more fully aware that I was going to die.

Q:

A: And that's when I woke up.

Twilford Baines, Buck Hunter Unbounded

Rifle season is ephemeral, lasting only a few blissful weeks, and Twilford, like his brothers and father, uncles and cousins, and generations of Baines preceding them, rose before sunlight and drove to the rural acreage of land where he'd become accustomed to spending this day, where deer were plentiful, where trees were dense enough to provide cover but not so thick as to prevent sight lines to his prey. He preferred to hunt alone. There was something sacred about the quiet pine air, the flickering of birds in branches the only disruption to the stillness.

On this particular morning, fog-headed and lethargic and emotionally spent, Twilford slipped a pinch of chew behind his lip and propped his orange-jacketed torso against a birch. The soil was frosty. He knew the area well, the landowner being an old friend of his deceased father, and he knew a trail that served as a thruway for the animals to reach the pond. Already he'd spotted tracks, some old, some recent, and so he positioned himself a good forty yards distant and hunkered in for a wait. To hunt required supreme patience and a monk-like stillness and silence. Not one to believe in the application of deer urine or other methods that seemed like trickery, he'd dulled his scent with a few sprays of pine essence. After all it wasn't hard to outwit a dumb animal. Twilford's true druthers was to bow hunt; however, a high school football injury had left a poorly healed tear in the muscles around his scapula, making it impossible to draw the string without intense discomfort. So bullets it was.

Twilford was having trouble staying awake. His head throbbed from the copious whiskey he'd guzzled mere hours ago. He felt at once numb and wretched, left this way by a personal issue of a magnitude he'd never experienced and didn't quite honestly know how to handle. The woman he'd been seeing for over a year—her name was Elsa; they had talked of marriage—had sat him at the table the previous night and told him, with a stern and placid face, that she loved another man. That the cuckolder was Jeremy, his closest friend of twenty years, seemed a tragedy of comical country song proportions, but the hurt was very real, deep, and debilitating. A double betrayal. She'd confessed with dry eyes that she'd been sleeping with his now ex-friend for upwards of three months, a quarter of the duration of her and Twilford's courtship.

Elsa had left him, officially and bodily anyway, because quite apparently she'd not been truly present for quite some time. She had only been an illusion, albeit a warm-bodied, soft, fragrant one. And when she was gone he'd lifted one bottle followed by another to his lips, getting so wasted he'd needed to throw up, at which point he'd throated two fingers and purged while slumped over the bowl. Though highly inebriated in the waning hours of night, he'd still made a point of setting his alarm before collapsing upon the mattress. He would not miss Opening Day just because of the cruelty he had suffered. If anything, a return to the woods and to the tradition he prized above all might provide at least a temporary balm to his scorched soul.

Against the tree he jerked awake, not realizing he'd fallen asleep. Juice had dribbled out of his mouth, spattering his pants brown. When he spasmed into consciousness he also tipped his Thermos, the lid of which wasn't properly secured. Coffee chugged out onto the ground beneath him. Pants wet, he stood and cursed. Was this, he thought, all to provide laughter to the man upstairs? When and why had he been appointed cosmic jester?

At that exact moment he heard the crack of branches, his eyes detecting a glimpse of movement. Two deer were cautiously proceeding along the feed run, nosing the soil and picking at the foliage with their teeth. Twilford arranged the binoculars and focused before locating the animals. A buck and a doe. They both had antlers but as was natural the buck's were the prize, a glorious rack. He counted seven points on one side, which doubled equaled fourteen, his head not too dogged for simple arithmetic. Sighting a pair like this, a buck and a doe, was a rarity. The doe usually stuck with her fawn while the buck ambled solo.

Twilford waited three full minutes as the pair inched past a wide oak and into a clearing. He raised the rifle and took aim at the buck, the crosshairs falling easily onto the animal's torso just behind the front leg. His finger trembled on the trigger. At the last moment, he redirected the barrel toward the doe. He fired, dropping her. The buck bolted.

He knew he'd done a bad thing. Does were off-limits during rifle season, a lost license and a heavy fine the penalty, not to mention scorn and derision from hunters who caught wind of the transgression. He regretted it, but now it was too late to fix.

He arm-wiped sweat from his eyes, re-loaded his gun, and put fresh chew to his gums before walking to the carcass. When he got to the spot where she'd fallen, the doe was gone. It had only been wounded.

He told himself to be calm. He had tracked wounded prey before, and often. In fact, Twilford had never left an injured deer in the wild, and had no reason to think this would break the precedent.

Blood had pooled where the creature buckled. He spotted additional drops a few feet away, in the direction of the pond. With rifle shouldered he followed the trail, stepping as fast as possible without raising a ruckus. Blood glinted on the leaves, on the dirt, as sunshine stabbed through the awning of trees.

He found her at the water's edge, prone on her side. He knelt beside the doe and touched her flank. Blood flowed gentle and dark from her nostrils. A peaceful feeling settled into Twilford. He hoped he could ease her transition, but then something beneath the hide jabbed dully against his hand. She was pregnant, the fawn still alive. He pulled the knife from his belt and sawed carefully, a flood of innards cascading as he worked her length. He reached in and took hold of a little beast, hairless and brownish-red and coated by the juices of the sac. On the ground it writhed, mouth issuing a plaintive gurgle, kicking for life but finding none. It was too small, and Twilford realized he should have left the thing in the warm comfort of his momma until its light faded. Another mistake, another death, and Twilford's hands bore the blood.

He rinsed in the pond and was about to head back to his Thermos and gun case when the buck rushed him. It charged headlong, all two hundred pounds barreling into Twilford, knocking him down and raking his face with its rack. One of the points punctured his neck, the thick hook of antler scratching his windpipe from the inside.

Then the buck was gone, clumping away through the brush as Twilford tried but failed to crawl. He lay beside his gun in the weeds. His chest was crushed; gasping for breath felt like inhaling fire. He knew if he didn't get help soon he would die. A gunshot wouldn't bring other hunters near; they would navigate away from wherever the sound came.

His cell phone was in his pants pocket. Wincing, pressing one hand to his bleeding neck, he managed to retrieve it. A signal, although weak, meant he could try.

He considered dialing 9-1-1—knowing this was the logical choice—but speaking with a faceless, anonymous operator during perhaps his last moments on earth was a thought as crushing as the pain in his chest. He needed to hear a familiar voice.

He realized, though, as if for the first time, that only two peoples' numbers were programmed into his phone: Elsa and Jeremy. A handful of other numbers were in there, too: but only restaurants with delivery service. How had he reached mid-life with but two friends? *Sadly* was the answer.

He dialed Elsa. He needed to at least profess something to her. Something...but what? Not love, exactly. Not anger, either. All of the rage seemed to have flowed out from the puncture in his neck. Had he failed her as a boyfriend? Surely, yes, although no specific failings entered his mind. But Elsa was a kind woman, a person of character who would not stray without cause; he bore at least a share of the blame.

He heard two rings. Then a young man's voice: "Duncan's Pizza, may I take your order?"

Twilford's thick thumb had pushed the wrong entry. He spoke: "Hello, I'm dying."

The worker chuckled. "Pretty hungry, huh? Well, what can we get you?"

Twilford considered. The thought of a hot pizza, the grease-pooled cheese and tangy sauce, made his stomach growl. His pain had settled into a dreamy numbness. He hadn't eaten anything today on account of the hangover, and now he was starving.

"Cajun Deluxe Meat Lovers. Extra large."

"Delivery or pickup?"

"First one."

"Delivery?"

"Mm hm."

"Anything to drink?"

Something important he had to tell this young man, but he was having trouble remembering. Twilford gathered air best he could and said, "No sausage."

"No sausage on the Cajun Deluxe Meat Lovers. Got it." The young man's voice was calm and comforting. Twilford pictured him as handsome and pleasant, with a nice smile. He would have a long, happy life. He would get married and raise good children. "Anything to drink?"

"Two-liter…Mountain Dew. Why not."

"All right, your total is $22.57. And what's the address?"

The edges of Twilford's vision blurred. Sunlight filtered through the trees and warmed his skin. "Pull over at the third mailbox on Haverty Road. Don't make any noise…" He coughed and felt blood in his mouth. "…The Nicholls' have a German Shepherd with a nasty temper…"

"Sir, our driver can't trespass on—"

"Walk until you get to the barbed wire fence. Go thirty paces south. There's a break in the fence. Crawl over it. Half a mile to the big oak tree—it's got a big knot near the base..."

"Sir, I don't think—"

"What's your name?"

"My name is Carl, but—"

"Carl, this is important. Find me, OK? I need this. Go past the tree and due west. Hit the mossy stump, you've gone too far."

"I need an actual street number or we can't deliver."

Daylight was fading. Was it dusk already? Twilford felt sleepy. His mouth was filling with something, maybe saliva. He tried to swallow but couldn't. A dark ring had encircled the sun, closing in with each passing second. His hunger flared like an ember in a gust, reminding him that he was, at least for this moment, still alive, still Twilford Baines, buck hunter.

"Now you wrote that I don't want sausage, right?"

Slice of Moon

The ugliest mystery of Bernie's wasn't revealed until the day we buried him. His soft, flat face, long and distant as a slice of moon, lead people to believe he was the type of man who'd exchanged doting glances with his high-school sweetheart for 45 years until her passing at the hands of some tragic ailment. His face conjured thoughts of contentment and slumber, like a pillow might do.

But as everyone knows, faces lie.

As far as anyone could tell, Bernie never even had a sweetheart, not in the conventional sense. None of us had the inclination or opportunity to ask Bernie why he remained a bachelor in the autumn years of his life, but before Larissa showed up on the palm of his hand like some precious stone, the speculation ranged from homosexuality to impotence to a monk-like need for solitude.

★

Bernie could have had a wife if he'd wanted one. Not that he was handsome. But Bernie did have a few qualities going for him. His hair rose up off his scalp like a cumulonimbus cloud. His teeth were wide, straight, and clean. Bernie didn't smoke, drink, or take the Lord's name in vain. Razor burn never reddened his neck (he couldn't grow facial hair). He was large but unimposing. Heavy but not powerful. A slow, easygoing man. Bernie reminded folks of a porch hound who's pleased to see a car pass every hour or two.

He also was like a Bachman's Sparrow—you might go out daily but only spot him every second year.

At a wedding reception at the VFW, for instance, while talking with Marty and Missy Lamb about the unfair scrutiny Doctor Strobe was receiving for his treatment practices, the nagging sensation of being watched might hit you, and there by your right shoulder would be Bernie, wearing a shy smile as if he knew he shouldn't sneak up but he plain didn't realize he was doing it until that scared expression appeared on your face.

The main feature that separated Bernie from other Gifford men was his hands. They were never measured, not even after he died, but it wouldn't be surprising to learn that they were a foot long, heel to fingertip. Bernie could palm three bottles of wine. And yet they weren't the kind of hands that frightened children. They were manicured and uncalloused, even womanly in spite of their size.

Bernie worked the Indiana Turnpike booth between Gary and South Bend for as long as there'd been a turnpike (1956). To Gifford folks, the job sounded strange—sitting on a stool in a box for eight hours a day, earning a paycheck. Having it as a temporary job was one thing, but a career was hard to understand. The Turnpike was, by far, the steadiest job Bernie had ever had. Sometimes, driving to Chicago, you saw him in his booth and said hello; sometimes you didn't say a word. Folks tossed their dimes and went on their way; it's human nature. He couldn't have minded.

The fumes, though, he should've minded. Most people you couldn't pay to work in that claustrophobic space. But Bernie did it for decades. Never late, never sick. He didn't visit Doctor Strobe once in fifty years. Blessed with perfect health. Only time he went to see Dr. Strobe was with Larissa, after she'd grown up and gotten herself pregnant.

★

Larissa was Bernie's special girl. That's what he called her.

The first one who ever saw Larissa was Smeets Folger. Smeets was alone in his donut shop at 5:00 a.m., rolling out trays of goodies for the morning rush. He'd lost his own little girl in a custody battle everyone remembers because of how his wife Ronette faked arm bruises and then left town.

Bernie had strolled into the shop and ordered a large decaf and a Long John. He didn't say a word about the tiny human laying asleep on the palm of his hand. Smeets figured the infant to be just days old, bundled in a newspaper. This was years ago. Bernie was forty-five, so even if the newspaper swaddle hadn't caught Smeets' attention, then the sight of this past-his-prime man carrying a baby on his palm when he'd never been seen in public with a woman was enough to arouse curiosity. Bernie paid with exact change, which was his way. He gathered coffee and donut in his free hand and walked out.

Other than their time in the tollbooth, Bernie and Larissa appeared in public exactly fifteen times over the next fifteen years.

Bernie came into town alone more often than that, but not much more. He lived on CR143, halfway to Beardstown and a quarter-mile from the Wright farm. We weren't afraid of an Ed Gein or anything like that. It's just that people like to know who's shopping at their grocery and passing their elementary school. And let's face it; everyone knows that a guy who doesn't date or marry is suspicious. Gifford didn't make that rule.

Still, Bernie could polite your socks off. Always held the door for whoever was behind him, even folks twenty steps back. When ticketed for driving with expired insurance, he shook hands with Sheriff Rhodes, thanked him for the job he was doing, and gave him a rhubarb pie. In the Piggly Wiggly, Bernie's cart was always loaded with 24-packs of Charmin and jars of mayonnaise the size of fire hydrants, which made sense considering how infrequently he came into town. He offered a smile to anyone who passed him in the aisle, such as Bonnie Mertz, a cashier.

Bonnie stood behind Bernie through it all. She even went on record during the trial: "He has the kind of eyes that make you forget what you're doing." She meant it as a compliment.

Seeing the gentle giant pushing baby Larissa along the sidewalk in a stroller, even once a year, endeared people to him. Red flags, though, had already been raised. First, there was the question of where and how he'd gotten this baby. Second, there was the question of his politeness, which was so blatant that it simply had to be covering up something sinister.

★

He didn't appear in Gifford by magic. His parents were hardworking Hoosiers who raised peas and corn near Beardstown. They gave Bernie a Christian upbringing. They encouraged him to play hoops at Hodges High School and cheered him on during games. Bernie started a chess club that never attracted more than three members. But at least he tried. He got the prettiest girl to agree to go to prom with him, although he never went through with it and instead sat in his room on prom night writing those peculiar nursery rhymes until his mother rapped on the door and told him to turn out the light.

He graduated with the other members of his class, and none of those thirty people recall Bernie doing anything weird or upsetting in high school or elementary school. Certainly he did nothing violent. Punctual, courteous, well-mannered, decent—these are the words classmates and teachers used to describe Bernie. In basketball, he led the team in assists. When pencils were needed for a test, Bernie stood first in line at the sharpener.

Glory wasn't Bernie's goal, which sounds admirable until you realize he didn't have any goals. None he shared with anybody, anyway. The overall impression Bernie made was very little impression; he was one of those people that no one is close to but also no one is so far from.

Bernie was in his twenties when the Indiana Road Commission stapled flyers on every telephone pole in town. They were trying to attract workers for the new toll road. Bernie signed right up. As he had no other skills, it probably seemed like a smart decision. He'd never taken to the plow, even though Bob and Betty had tried every manner to entice him to work the farm. They'd wanted a big brood, but Bernie's cesarean delivery had damaged Betty's uterus, and she couldn't bear more children. Hiring outside help was going to be necessary whether or not Bernie joined the family business, so his folks didn't pressure him.

The tide turned for Bernie when his dad got the bone cancer. By the time Doctor Strobe made the diagnosis, it had already spread. Bernie had just been hired by the Road Commission, and though his mother begged, he wouldn't quit the tollbooth to help run the farm. To lots of people, this was strike number one.

Larissa is a woman now, a mother herself. At last check, she was living in the Florida Keys, far from the Gifford folks who witnessed her childhood like a slide show, tiny increments that leapt forward in time by the year. We don't know if she's married, nor do we know the health of her daughter. What we do know is that Larissa was absent from Bernie's funeral. This was strike number three.

★

Strike number two was a big one. It was the kind of act that even a mother might not forgive. By the time Bernie committed it, however, his own mother was dead. She fell to breast cancer in 1965, when Bernie was pushing forty. At her funeral, those huge hands of his covered his face. He sobbed like a baby. He couldn't walk except in a lurching stagger like a drunk. Those of us who'd known his momma attended the wake and burial. The sight of Bernie made us sick with pity, but not the kind of pity that makes you want to help. It only makes you feel uncomfortable. So everyone hung back and left him alone.

Before long he was drinking a pint of vodka a day, and it wasn't two months later when the pint became two.

For seven years, Bernie became a ghost. Only visible in the window of that tollbooth, or at the liquor store. He didn't look good. Seemed ill, sun-starved. Nobody inquired after his health.

And then he appeared at the counter of Smeets' doughnut shop with a newborn baby in his hand.

★

Strike two was Bernie's decision to homeschool Larissa.

And what about his job? Did he arrange to have child care?

No. He brought that poor child into the toll booth. That's where they had their lessons. The toll booth is where that girl was educated, where she ate her school lunches, where she grew up. Nobody knows how he convinced his employers to support this arrangement; no more than anyone knows if Bernie led his daughter in the Pledge of Allegiance each morning. Setting aside concerns about the quality of the public education system, was it healthy and right to keep her like a prisoner, away from other children, in that fishbowl of exhaust fumes by the side of the highway?

The murmurs began. Qualities of Bernie's that had been sympathetic, or at least innocuous, took on a darker tint. His smiles at the Piggly Wiggly seemed to hide a secret. Sheriff Rhodes no longer accepted his pies. The nursery rhymes no longer read as quirky or endearing:

Big Willy Walker never worked the farm
Stared at the sky praying for rain
When Willy fell into the well

He thought he found the way to Hell
But really he just knocked out his brains.

On grocery runs Bernie gave his poems to the grocery clerk Bonnie, scrawled on lined paper that had been torn from a notebook. Handed them across the counter with a sly nod. Bonnie kept them all.

Murmurs gain volume if left unchecked, and unchecked these were. Bernie did nothing to ease suspicions or answer questions—not that anybody asked him directly, but if a person's social radar is even moderately functional he ought to anticipate questions even when they aren't spoken to his face.

Once Larissa reached high school age, the whispers got real loud. Something unnatural and unseemly about an old single man and a teenage girl living alone, keeping completely to themselves. The biggest question was whether Bernie was actually Larissa's biological father. Snooping around Gifford records turned up nothing that would answer this question. Sheriff Rhodes responded to pressure and called around to neighboring county hospitals and adoption agencies. Did they have any record of the birth of a little girl around such-and-so time? Any record of a newborn white baby girl being adopted?

I don't need to tell you that Sheriff's searches came up empty. This was the opposite of good news for Bernie.

★

Sadly, it's not difficult to locate a cold case of a kidnapped infant girl somewhere in the United States.

None were found in the immediate vicinity of Gifford, Indiana, no. Nor in the region of the Great Lakes. Look hard enough, though, and one will turn up.

Way down south in the city of Biloxi, Mississippi, a baby had gone missing precisely fifteen years earlier.

★

It didn't help that Bernie's house looked like a dead zone. Gray weathered clapboard siding, windowsills and gutters sagging, a cobblestone chimney one stiff breeze from avalanche. A pair of half-dead apple trees hunched like old arthritic ladies near a shack that had caved-in and surrendered to weeds. Crows picking at road kill in the gravel. The land hadn't been tilled in years; hadn't even been tended. The yard got mowed on occasion, which saved the home from seeming abandoned, and from the road a passerby could sometimes see a warm light glowing above the kitchen table, where two figures shared a meal in the early hours of dusk.

★

During the hearing the courtroom was filled to burst.

Larissa, still a minor, was not required to take the stand. She elected to do so anyway. Most folks hadn't ever heard her speak. She'd grown into a tall, primly dressed young lady with straight sandy hair. Her voice was deeper than one might expect from a girl her age. Freckled cheeks, sun-kissed skin. Did she go outside a lot? That would have been a surprise.

People had begun imagining all sorts of horrors inside that house. Torture chambers, shackles, raw meat, and of course the unspoken nightmares of sexual deviancy that haunted everybody's dreams.

By Larissa's testimony, which everyone admitted was lucid and confident, hardly the demeanor of a torture victim, she'd been raised well, taken good care of, fed and clothed and educated up to all apparent standards. She'd been inspected, too, by the social workers. No signs of abuse or mistreatment.

DNA tests were still new and expensive, so the case against Bernie amounted to circumstantial speculation. Could anybody say whether he had or had not driven down to Biloxi, Mississippi on this random evening fifteen years prior?

Could any witness place him in that city at the time of the crime? Was there any physical evidence that connected Bernie to the scene?

No answered all of them. The baby had been snaked right out of her crib, the kidnapper entering through an open window between 2:00 a.m. and 5:00 a.m. There wasn't a trail from Bernie or anyone: no fingerprints, clothing fibers, footprints, or tire tracks. It's the reason the case went cold in the first place.

The parents of the kidnapped baby drove all the way up to Gifford. They'd gone on and had three more kids after their first one vanished, so most folks didn't have a whole lot of pity for them. They brought pictures of the baby, and the prosecutor showed them next to Larissa's face.

Bernie didn't have any photos of Larissa as a baby. Not a single one. That was suspicious as hell, but hardly evidence of a kidnapping.

Still, the police had a suspect. A very good one, promising. A girl who appeared mysteriously in Gifford at the same time that baby went missing. Coincidences like that just didn't happen.

Can you prove who your parents are? Sure, you've got a neatly typed birth certificate that names your momma and daddy. But that isn't proof, is it? Legal proof maybe, but not any other kind. You just elect to believe it.

You have to study your momma's face, eyes, nose; you watch your hairline as you age and compare it to your daddy's. It's all circumstantial evidence. How do you really *know*? Even if you used modern-day paternity technology, let's be honest: you trust what the guys in the lab coats are telling you.

Truth is nobody possesses 100% certainty about who they are, where they came from, how they came into this world. The only fact you can know is that you don't know.

★

Had we done a good thing? Had we saved that girl? Is it even possible to save someone who doesn't believe they're in trouble?

One girl disappears without a trace. A mystery unsolved. One girl appears like magic. Another mystery. Is this the way the universe keeps in balance?

★

Only one person could truly answer the question of where Larissa came from.

Bernie entered a plea of not guilty to the charges of kidnapping across state lines, a federal offense. Then he refused to testify. He was dressed in a brown three-piece suit nobody had seen since his father wore it to church years ago. Cornflower blue polyester tie. The loafers on his feet were dulled with dust.

He was urged to take the stand. Spectators yelled at him, saying "Get on up there and tell us you didn't do it," but he only stared straight ahead, no emotion visible, just that slice of moon face as distant as ever. The judge called for order and smacked his gavel down.

Why didn't Bernie lay his hand on the Bible and set himself free? Or at least try?

Most folks interpreted his silence as a sure sign of guilt.

"Only a man's got something to hide doesn't come out and give his side of the story," Missy Lamb said.

"He can't swear to tell the truth because the truth'll put him behind bars," Becky Foster said.

Jury didn't see it that way, though. They spent three weeks deliberating on the strange and tangled situation, only to file back in and announce that they were unable to reach a decision. They were as hung as the American flag outside the courtroom. Bernie was free to go.

Larissa left Gifford not even a year later. Around that time a kid didn't have to finish high school if they didn't want, and she was a legal adult by age sixteen according to Indiana law. Nobody missed her, of course, because she'd always been a ghost in Gifford. However, it didn't make anyone happy either. It just confirmed what everyone already knew: that Bernie'd been keeping her against her will all these years, and at first chance she flew out the door faster than a mouse out of a potato sack.

Bernie had the mark on him then. No one gave him the time of day. Aged real fast. Retired from his tollbooth job, had his weekly groceries delivered. More or less vanished from Gifford just like his daughter.

Not too many years later, Dale the grocer's son showed up on Bernie's porch and smelled the corpse, expired for a week at his kitchen table. His wrists were cut open, blood soaking into the old oak table.

His death was discussed over coffees at Corvette Café.

"Could have done it later. Like wait 'til the day before poor Dale come drop off the groceries. Wouldn't have stunk so bad."

"Probably you're right he planned it that way."

"Revenge from beyond the grave."

"Memorial service and burial tomorrow."

"You going?"

"Guess maybe. Don't help to hold grudges against the dead."

"Supposed to be paying respects. Don't figure many got respect to pay."

"Why you think that girl never said a bad word about him?"

"Seemed like she genuinely loved him. That's how I saw it."

"Kid never knew any different. Whatever life he gave her was the only one she had."

"I never knew any different, and I still found a way to hate my daddy."

"Hahaha, he wasn't so bad."

"You didn't live with him."

"Ever think Bernie was innocent?"

"Wouldn't say if I did."

"You got enough enemies."

"I'll tell you what. If his sin was raising up a good, smart young lady like that, then there's worse to be guilty of."

"I heard she's down in Florida, going to college. Got her own youngster."

"That right?"

"Jerry's nephew's at the community college down Lakeland. She's in one of his classes."

"Bless her heart."

"Guess she was too good for Gifford."

"Bernie thought he was, too."

"No, that wasn't the shape of him."

"That's right. Bernie's always been lukewarm water, you ask me."

"Neutral men are the devil's allies."

★

Respected or not, Bernie's memorial drew record crowds. Bodies filed into the Earl Funeral Home on a blistering day in August, fans and handkerchiefs waving and dabbing. Guess we all wanted one last glimpse to make sure he was really gone. He'd been such a fixture for so many years, like that abandoned barn marking the final stretch of highway before reaching Gifford.

He was dressed in the same brown suit and cornflower blue tie as at the trial. The gigantic hands folded over his chest seemed artificial, like pieces carved from granite, his long pale face no more peaceful and untroubled than it had been while blood ran through his veins. Soft Christian hymns played. People piled flowers around the casket because even the questionable among us deserve beauty at their going-away.

But Bernie had one more message for Gifford. Folks filing past the open coffin inevitably paused, studying that moon face for longer than occasion demanded.

People began leaning in, lifting their glasses in disbelief. Now and then you could hear a gasp. Before long conspiratorial whispers circulated through the gathered, faces rumpled in dismay.

Mike Earl denied doing anything to give Bernie that expression. But everyone will tell you that it was there, undeniable: a smirk on those lips. A Mona Lisa grin suggestive of pleasures and pains none of us poor fools could ever understand.

The Source of All Feeling

"Jake, this is impossible." Loren pretended to pour a glass of wine at the bureau by the window. "I cannot carry on with a married man this way. You have to leave her or let me go. It's your choice!" She guzzled the imaginary burgundy.

Jake lay shirtless on the unmade bed with an unlit cigarette dangling out of his mouth. "I always said you were a little firecracker. Now get over here and give me a handful."

"Stop! Stop, stop, stop!" The director clomped up the steps onto the stage.

"What was wrong with that?" the actor playing Jake said.

"It wasn't you, it wasn't you."

"What, me?" the woman said.

"You, you." The director's arms waved like a drowning man's. "I need to see you use that neck more."

"My neck?"

"*My neck?* Of course your neck! How can you give the truth of this situation without using your neck?"

"What do you recommend I do with it?"

"What do necks do?"

"I don't know. Turn?"

"Turn." The director chuckled. "*Heads* turn. Cars turn when you have to go to the market for bread. Little kittens turn when they hear loud sounds. Aw, aren't they so cute?" He smashed his thigh with an open palm. "Necks decide everything! Now let's do it again with much less subtlety in the neck. OK?"

The actors resumed their positions and resituated the props.

"Jake, this is impossible." Loren poured a glass of wine at the bureau. "I cannot carry on with a married man this way. You have to leave her or let me go. It's your choice!" She guzzled the wine and slammed the glass onto the bureau.

"I always said you were a little firecracker. Now get over—"

"Stop!" The director stormed up the steps. He stood uncomfortably close to his actors when giving them notes.

"I used my neck a lot more," the woman said. "It felt right."

"Yes, dear. Your neck was perfect, much more dynamic. This is not about your neck." He turned to the man on the bed. "You!"

"Me?"

"Tell me, is your whole self immersed in this moment?"

The man glanced at the woman, frowning.

"Don't check with her. Answer yourself!"

"I—yes. My whole self. I *am* Jake. One hundred percent."

"Then why is your back so lifeless?"

"My back?"

"Back, spinal cord, whatever you want to call it! Please, let's not argue semantics! We have only two days until opening!"

"OK, I hear you. What can I do better?"

"*Involve* your back." The director smacked his forehead. "Duh! Why would you only bring your front side into this situation? Huh? You, you, you—I'm talking to the actor now. I'm not talking to Jake anymore. Do *you* go about your day forgetting completely about your spine? Come on, don't kid me!"

The man rubbed his nose thoughtfully. "Yes, I see what you mean. Can we do it again?"

"What a concept!" The director tilted his condescending smile toward the woman, who was practicing neck moves. "Places again!"

"Jake, this is impossible. I cannot carry on with a married man this way. You have to leave her or let me go. It's your choice!"

"I always said you were a little firecracker. Now get over here and give me a handful."

"God! Why, why, why? What is going on today? Have I woken in a dream? Am I working with zombies? Feel my arms! Feel them!"

The woman felt the director's bare arms.

"Goosebumps!" he cried. "Not because I'm moved to tears but because I'm frightened!"

"Frightened of what?" the woman asked. Her voice had a hopeful tone. "Are we approaching some bigger truth?" She raised her eyebrows at her co-star. "I felt something that time. We're getting close. My soul sort of shifted when you said your lines."

The man on the bed gave her a thumbs-up and mouthed "Thank you."

"What?!" The director paraded around the stage, flailing and screaming. He returned to the man's side and pointed a finger inches from his face. "Are you a robot?"

"I've been saying the lines this way every time. I thought you liked it."

"Not the lines, dummy. The lids." He pulled his own eyes open comically wide. "This is what I see when I look at you. Big eyeballs, big naked eyeballs."

"You want me to close my eyes? Squint, maybe?" He narrowed his eyelids dramatically.

"Ha ha ha, very witty." He kicked the mattress and yelled, "No! Why do you people torment me?" He approached the woman and placed a gentle hand on her shoulder. "Dear, can you please tell him what he should do with his eyelids?"

The woman considered for a moment. "Bring them into the scene?"

"Bingo! Give her the million-dollar prize!" He mimed tossing dollar bills at her before redirecting his attention to the man. "Yes, *please* don't be that person. Do you want the audience out there to say, *He said his lines all right, but did you see his eyelids? It's like he just got them yesterday!* You'll be laughed right out of the theater community, pal. Activate them! Activate them!"

The man nodded, ashamed. He sat on the edge of the bed and put his face in his hands. The woman walked over and gave him a hug.

"I hope he's consoling you, too, little lady," the director said.

"Yes, it's been a long day," she said.

"Long day," the director scoffed. "In that last run-through: Do you really think you convinced me that you are in love with this man? That you are prepared to destroy his family, take him away from his children, be branded a home wrecker in the community, lose your job at the church, betray your best friend, acquire a sexually transmitted disease—for this true, eternal love? Do you believe that you conveyed all of this in that single moment?"

Her expression crumpled. She shook her head, using her neck perfectly.

"Good," said the director quietly. "Now for the tough part. Can you tell me what you need to do?"

Tears streamed down her face. "My arms," she whimpered.

"Oh my sweet, sweet lady. You are learning. But no. Not your arms. Your elbows."

"But my elbows are part of my arms, aren't they? That's what they taught me in acting school."

The director clapped his hands sharply, the noise echoing through the dark, empty theater. "Wonderful!" he yelled. "I'm so very happy to hear that the gatekeepers of the dramatic arts are leading our young thespians to believe that the *elbow* is *part of the arm*! Unbelievable!" He fell on the floor laughing. A minute later he propped himself on his own elbow. "Tell me: Is the Earth merely *a part of the universe*?"

"I—um. Yes?"

"Waahahaha! OK, so you live, breathe, love, fuck, and eat—where? On *a part of the universe*? Is that what you tell your friends?"

"No, I mean, I'm on the Earth. Living and fucking. Of course."

"Show me what your arms look like with no elbows! Show me!" He crouched on the stage like a panther.

The man on the bed was sobbing with noisy mucus as the woman got to her feet and held her arms straight at her sides. She too was blubbering.

"Do you feel like a fool? Do you?"

"Yes!"

"Because you look like one! A fool with no elbows!"

"Yes!"

"Oh, you've got *arms* all right. Don't you? Hey, check out the lady with the arms, everyone! Don't you want to throw away your whole life just to be with her?"

"No, no, oh god, no!"

"What's the problem, huh? I thought all you needed were arms to get you through the day!"

"Leave her alone!" the man screamed. He launched from the bed flapping his eyelids madly.

"She is already alone," the director answered in a somber whisper. "As are you, as am I. Look around." He spread his arms and faced the empty seats, stepping to the edge of the stage as if to embrace the entire world. "No one has been to this theater in years. Why would they come here to be shown human emotion mimed for their amusement? The people out there are no fools, and we will not be fools either. Whatever is inside us must be dug out with a claw hammer." His voice trembled; he perched near the darkness, half in light.

When he turned again to his actors, his eyes seemed to have been swallowed. "We will dig until we find the source of all feeling. Now take your places again."

Snow, Lightly Falling

Ladies and gentlemen, I am delighted to welcome you to the one and only performance of Mitchell Miracle and his Cakes of Instruction!

[Enthusiastic applause and whistling]

Many of you are still settling into your seats, and I will use this opportunity to remind you that all photography, as well as video and audio recording, are prohibited during the performance. You should, in fact, have remitted all electronic devices, in addition to personal effects like purses, wallets, car keys, eye liner, old receipts, bank statements, lip balm, candy, and rape whistles to the gentlemen at the door. Those two guys were hard to miss, am I right?

[Chuckles and supportive claps]

To be completely serious for a moment: those two men, whom some of you no doubt found intimidating and perhaps even unsettling to look at, do in fact have names. They are Feck and Fennel, and as you affirmed with your own eyes, they are identical twins. Nature has inflicted them with the disorder known in the vernacular as gigantism, which is why their bodies are so humongous. Ah, it's a remarkable and mysterious force, Nature.

[Wild roars of joy]

Feck and Fennel will be playing a key role in tonight's event, in addition to the important duty of depositing your belongings into those metal buckets. These abnormally tall boys—because you see, they are in fact only seventeen years of age, on the cusp of manhood—have volunteered to consume the Cakes of Instruction before your very eyes.

[Gasps and laughter]

For your amusement, yes of course. For what other reason should we be gathered on this lovely evening? This stage, the seats in which you titter, the theater, the world itself—all of this was constructed for your amusement and entertainment, to provide each man, woman, and child the much-needed escape from the shackles of day-to-day life. Truly, there is no greater purpose in life than to seek smiles, am I right? And such a rarity they are in these troubled times.

When you look in the mirror, how many of you see beauty? How many recognize the sublime in your own visage? How many notice the true, complex machinery of humanity, the soul of an individual spirit as alive and precious and necessary as the sun in the afternoon sky?

[Nervous murmurs and scattered boos]

Mitchell Miracle and the Cakes of Instruction will be appearing shortly. The lights, please.

[House lights dim; stage spotlight creates a circle of illumination on the bare wood]

[People lean forward in their seats; stiff air of anticipation]

[A crying baby is quickly hushed]

[Typhoons, wildfires, and earthquakes rage {distantly, providing cosmic balance}]

[The scent of pancakes wafts into the crowd]

Ah, yes. Breathe that smell. Smell that breath. Mitchell Miracle has worked his way inside you. Quite literally, his Cakes of Instruction are entering your bodies. Chemical alterations in your brain, causing you to salivate, to squirm in your seats with hunger. If we're quiet, I'll bet we can hear the deep grumble of your collective stomachs, yearning for satisfaction. I'll bet we can hear the veins in your arms dancing, the bones in your feet twisting with pleasure, the flutter of your brainstem as it shivers in a pool of delight and terror.

[Weary applause, some quiet sobbing]

And now we will begin the event. Allow me to stop being excited as we welcome Feck and Fennel.

[Feck and Fennel emerge from Stage Right, the clump-clump-clump of their shoes the only sound as they drag their tired bodies, battling the dark force of gravity]

I feel like a child next to these boys. It's not a bad feeling, if I may be honest. We all have a desire to return to the un-jaded days of youth. Observe how Feck and Fennel stand perfectly motionless as if etched from rock. Each of their heads is as vertically long as my forearm! Each hand can grip two footballs at once! Not that they are able to play sports, unfortunately. Physical activity puts quite a strain on their bodies, as you can imagine. Doctors say that they don't have long to live, which is a major reason they will be consuming the Cakes. The suits they are wearing were specially made for this evening, and don't they look nice?

[Cautious belches followed by coughs of delight]

Now the moment we have dreamed has arrived. Let us all rise and place our hands on our hearts as the Cakes of Instruction are brought before us.

[A wheeled cart enters from Stage Left, bearing two pancakes on a plate. The person pushing the cart appears to be made of clear sky.]

This is Mitchell Miracle, and he would prefer that you do not look at him. He is required, naturally, to escort the Cakes of Instruction onto the stage—after all, this is his duty and his privilege—but nothing would bring him more internal pain and consternation than the crowd's eyes assaulting him during this private, vulnerable experience.

Feck and Fennel, I can assure you, have never seen these pancakes before. Isn't that correct, boys?

[Feck and Fennel remove their suits and underclothes, revealing a wilderness of flesh. Their clothing is whisked away by a sudden breeze. Pants, shirts, and coats dance above the audience like ghosts, rising into the darkness of the rafters.]

Now, have any of you in the audience seen these particular pancakes before?

[Eleven hands. These people are escorted from the auditorium weeping tears of joy.]

As you all know, we do not have a drummer in this production. So I will ask each of you to please imagine a drum roll, one that is tight and loud, one that builds anticipation into mania and vibrates your insides like a hurricane shakes a flagpole. Or if you would prefer, you could imagine a section of violins, violas, and cellos playing staccato notes in unison, vibrating your insides once again like a hurricane shaking a flagpole. Or you may simply imagine the flagpole. Any of these options will suffice.

[Audience snoozes comfortably, dreaming of salamanders and knives]

Now, Feck. Now, Fennel. Tender giants of the night. Would you do the honors of selecting a cake for each other? There, do you each have one? Are you certain of your choices? Very well. Please examine the cakes. Look at them closely and be sure that they are well-cooked, warm to the touch, the color of dying corn, the color of fever. There, yes. Place them into each other's mouths. Open wide. And wider. Breathe softly and caress one another's cheeks as your mother once did.

[Feck and Fennel have become trees, lean and sturdy, timeless]

[A light snow begins to fall, covering the sleeping audience]

[Hand-in-hand, the buckets of personal items exit the theater, accompanied by a somber wind]

[Curtain]

Outline

"Please lie down," the man said. He gestured at the pale sidewalk pocked with little divots.

"What for?" asked the boy. Could he trust this man? This stranger?

"I can't draw your outline unless you're on the ground, can I?" A smile curled the man's lips; his eyes sparkled.

He was younger than the boy's father. Better looking, slim and athletic. Carried himself with a bright and bouncy step. Dressed in khaki shorts and a blue shirt the color of the afternoon sky. The boy had been reading on a bench in front of the library, waiting for his father to get out of his doctor's appointment down the block.

"Jack London," the man said, nodding at the book. "Man versus nature, am I right?"

The boy closed the book, embarrassed. Reading was his own private experience, and he didn't like talking about it. Not to anyone, not even his parents. "Man doesn't usually come out on top in that battle." He threw back his head and gave a robust chuckle, as if he'd made a great joke. His blond hair was as bouncy as his step.

"Like I said," the man continued. "I'm doing an art project. Kind of an experiment, actually. What kid doesn't like experiments?"

He set his case on the sidewalk. It looked like a suitcase, rectangular, bound in dark leather the color of a storm cloud. The man unsnapped a button. Kneeling, he spread his wares, revealing an extensive collection of chalk. Each piece was strapped individually to the inside of the case.

"My own personal rainbow," the man said. "Pretty much every color you can think of."

The boy's curiosity was piqued. He'd been warned not to talk to strangers, but this man seemed kind. Other people—families—strolled along the sidewalks on this sunny warm day, peering into shops, licking ice cream cones. The boy felt safe, and he was enjoying the attention from the man. He didn't have any close friends. When your parents were both ill, kids didn't like to play with you.

"Take one," the man said. "Whichever one you want, it's yours."

The boy selected a piece the color of blood. It was nearly as thick as his wrist, and as long as a pencil. "I can have this?"

Seeing the boy admire it, the man said, "You won't find this at the local art supply store. This is special chalk, the only kind like it in the world."

"Where did you get it?"

The man's expression was thoughtful but guarded, as if remembering an event he wasn't sure he wanted to share. "I've had it for a long time, put it that way. Got it when I was around your age."

The man said they needed to relocate so nobody would step on the boy or bump him while he was tracing. Around the back of the library the two found a square of pavement close to the dumpsters. From this vantage the boy could no longer see the sidewalk.

"Don't worry," the man said, noticing the boy's concern. "Won't take long." He opened his case again and slid on a pair of gloves. "Were you waiting for someone?"

"My dad. He'll be back soon."

"He left you at the library?"

"He's at the doctor's," the boy said. "Should I lie down here?"

"Looks like a good spot. Nice and clean."

"I can't think of a pose." The boy was sitting on the pavement, suddenly at a loss, suddenly weighted by the inevitabilities and possibilities of life, which he was only now beginning to recognize.

"When someone walks past your outline, what should people think about? Anything you want to be, we'll make you come alive."

"Flying, I guess."

"Wonderful. A common request."

The boy lay on his stomach. He extended his hands and tried to imagine he was soaring through the sky. But the un-giving cement, rough against his bare arms, made him terribly aware that he was stuck to the earth.

"You thinking about your dad?"

"I don't know."

"He sick?"

For the past few months the father had been having dizzy spells. It was hard for him to take deep breaths. The boy's mother had an advanced case of MS and couldn't walk or move well. She'd been suffering for years, since the boy could remember. The boy tried not to think about what would happen if he lost his dad.

The man began chalking. The boy could feel the pressure of the man's hand against his ribs, wiggling back and forth as he drew a thick line. The raw scraping of the chalk sounded small and lonely. The concrete was cool against the boy's cheek. He imagined the man cutting a hole in the world. The boy would drop through it, leaving a space in the shape of him. He wanted to experience falling. He wanted to be pulled toward something terrible and permanent where bodies didn't exist. "To Build a Fire" was the story he had just finished. The man froze at the end. It was sad, but everybody dies. That's what the boy read.

The man worked without speaking, a steady pace, as if completing the outline was both necessary and urgent. It was a strange and unfamiliar sensation, someone working so diligently for him. It gave the boy a feeling in his stomach he'd never had before. The man progressed around the boy, doing the arms, hands, and head. The boy breathed in the man's body: rich salty sweat mixed with the dust of the chalk. Pressed against the pavement, the boy became aroused. Before long the man's hands were positioned inside the boy's thighs: back and forth, back and forth, jiggling the boy slightly but persistently. His erection strained. A powerful surge rushed through him. He gasped, feeling his own hot breath as he kissed the pavement.

"All done," the man said. "Let me help you up." He extended a hand.

The boy stood on his own. Wetness on his belly. He hoped the man hadn't seen, didn't know. The man's face gave no indication. The boy slid the gifted chalk into his pocket.

The man stepped back a few feet and looked hard at the outline, as if searching deep water for something he was certain lay just beyond his vision. "What do you think?"

The boy was shocked by what he saw: "It's me."

The man had used vibrant colors, lines weaving through each other, intertwining in a braid. The effect was of a pulsing energy, like a force field in the boy's shape. The boy couldn't believe how big he'd gotten.

A faraway voice called his name. The boy ran to his father without looking back, the blood-red chalk nestled firmly against his thigh.

Sanguine

Outside my office window is a green dumpster. All four of the businesses in this building use it.

This is my everyday view, this little parking lot at the edge of an overgrown baseball diamond.

Throughout the day smokers step outside and prop open the building's metal security door. They can't see me. At least I don't think they can. They never look at me.

I like to watch their awkward flirtations, their posing while they exhale. I like to watch the solo smokers puff away while thumbing their phones. The ending is always the same: cigarettes are mashed against the brick wall and flicked into the dumpster. The door slams.

Sanguine

I produce web copy for a Midwest chain of long-term care facilities. I used to write the copy. Now I supervise tech writers—three men, one woman—who handle the grunt work. I'm essentially the editor, the guy who puts a final stamp of approval on phrases such as "Your loved ones will enjoy 24-hour access to an exercise room featuring light barbells and state-of-the-art treadmills."

We had a healthy debate about the term *state-of-the-art* as a descriptor for our treadmills. We don't want to make any promises we can't keep, yet we need this world to sound idyllic, beyond reality. It's a delicate balance between truth and *other*.

I smoked for twenty-five years. Recently I had to quit because my wife is pregnant. She's younger than me by a couple of decades. People tend to think our age difference is scandalous until they meet her. Then they understand that she's the sort of person who was forty by the time she turned twenty. Nothing titillating about it.

So now I'm going to be a dad. I can't say it thrills me, the idea. Lately I've been reading our website and thinking, *that sounds kind of nice*. Sitting around on benches in a grassy area, shaded by oaks, tossing bread to pigeons. Playing checkers. I'd be the hot young man in the kennel, comparatively, surrounded by lonely old ladies. You could find worse ways to wind down your spin cycle, that's for sure.

My wife's mother is a resident in one of our homes. That's how I met her. My wife, that is. She filed a lawsuit against our company for false advertising. She said our website implied we would provide vegetarian options at every dinner.

Her mom's not even a vegetarian. But when my wife found out there weren't always meat-less options, she litigated. The judge agreed that the language was misleading. He seemed annoyed, however, that the issue didn't affect my wife personally. He didn't award any damages. He ordered us to revise the web copy. My reputation was dinged.

But I couldn't help falling in love with the lady with the giant glasses. During the hearing I became accustomed to gazing at her frowning face—so impassioned, so focused. My first wife lacked such qualities, or else she said I lacked them, I can't remember. That was a while ago.

My mother-in-law loves the meatloaf at Valley Glen Estates.

Sanguine

The last couple weeks I've noticed a homeless guy. He seems to favor our dumpster. Spends ten minutes a day on his tiptoes, reaching in there, examining one piece of garbage at a time. He'll pull up a crushed juice box and study it like an ancient relic before eventually tossing it back. What's he searching for?

When the smokers come out he slinks away with his plastic bags of who-knows-what.

Our baby is a girl. I taped her ultrasound photo to the side of my computer. Everyone in the office gushes about it, about her. My wife told me to tape it up there. Personally, I'm uncomfortable that people are staring at my daughter in this, her most private of spaces. Like voyeurs. She has no idea she's being photographed. How fair is that?

I really want to smoke.

I chew Orbit Bubblemint at every waking moment. Each paycheck is $100 lighter because of this gum. My jaw is like a gym rat's thigh. I'm no good with metaphors, which is why I quit writing stories. I realize my deficiencies, most of them anyway, which people tell me is an admirable trait. I have my doubts.

The homeless guy is pawing around in the dumpster one morning. On the Internet the world is abuzz about how rotten some new comic book movie is. People are threatening violence over it. My baby daughter is one month from breathing air. The homeless guy's beard looks like brown cotton candy. That's a pretty spot-on metaphor.

I've never seen him actually keep anything from our dumpster. Today is no exception. He must get pleasure from foraging. I've read about people like that.

No one should become a new parent at my age. I'm old enough that I despise seeing photos of myself. I've kept myself in decent shape, and even still, it looks like I have breasts. Very small breasts, but God, it's weird. Balding and breasted. Women don't grow penises. Mustaches, I guess, some of them. Fair enough.

The writers I supervise call me sir. I never asked them to. They know I quit smoking so they don't invite me to join them. In fact, they can't stop congratulating me for quitting. I say, *Really?*

My boss tells me I should regulate their breaks. He says smokers get away with slacking off. I tell him they're going to die soon. I'm kidding, he knows.

Sanguine

I let them smoke whenever they want.

Eight months into her pregnancy, my wife is nimbler than ever. I don't get it. She's doing yoga, contorting and squatting, bearing this huge protrusion that houses our daughter. She says it will relax the baby, and furthermore it will relax herself when she endures labor, which she intends to face without the help of pain-killing drugs. She's way stronger than I've ever been. Some days I wonder if that's a good thing.

Her cravings now include butter. Two or three pats at dinnertime seem to satiate her, although I still see her eyeing the tub when she thinks I'm not looking.

One week before the due date, I bum a cigarette from one of my tech writers. A male one. Tech writer, that is. It feels unseemly to bum a smoke from a woman. It might be interpreted the wrong way. These are the sorts of considerations one has to make as a supervisor.

As I'm smoking I'm keenly aware of how rested my jaw feels. The deadly carcinogens are delicious mixed with the trace Bubblemint flavor.

I look beyond the parking lot at the baseball diamond, such a sad sight. Hairy with weeds.

Littered with beer cans. The baselines are still visible, but barely. It's tough to look at without imagining the way it was meant to be, full of life.

When I'm finished I squash the cigarette until there is no ember. I flick it into the dumpster.

Before heading back inside, I also drop the ultrasound photo in there.

Later, I'm going to watch the homeless guy paw through the garbage.

I need to see if he takes my daughter's picture. I need to see if this is what he's been searching for all this time.

Scoundrels Among Us

Five scoundrels rolled into town in the biggest, blackest, loudest pickup folks had ever known. Tires tall as corn in full bloom, exhaust thunderous as the Devil's flatulence, the truck pancaked a dozen parked cars on its way to City Hall, where the driver cut the engine and four riders sprung from its bed: men carved from boulders; shirtless, foul-mouthed, and bent on destruction.

They entered screaming for the Mayor's head. The security guard was a wiry senior citizen with a hearing aid who hadn't been in a fistfight since basic training in the 1960s. He was nervous but figured himself capable of ousting ne'er-do-wells.

"You fellas need shirts to get in here." He nodded to a sign on the door that backed him up, confident this would do the trick.

One of the scoundrels lifted the security guard using a single hand. He spun the confused elder above his head before chucking him into a garbage can. The guard moaned upside-down until one of the men rolled the can into the street where, humiliated and nauseous, he sobbed and pondered retirement.

"We're taking this town!" yelled the head scoundrel. "We're taking the world!" All of the scoundrels were hulking and densely muscled, but this fellow was a head taller than the rest. Reflected fluorescent bulbs glowed like ghostly vapors on the flesh of his bald Caucasian skull. In his eyes blazed a reptilian intelligence: brutal and instinctive. He bore a mouthful of terrible gray teeth, and spit swung from his lips like a bulldog. The grunts and growls resounding deep within the cage of his chest suggested a beastly soul craving escape.

The scoundrels longed to defy gravity and fly up to the third floor where the Mayor's office was located—and their raging adrenaline made them feel fully capable—but Nature's laws dictated using the stairs. They stomped and screamed the whole way. Any poor fool who happened to be in their path was bowled over or karate-chopped into submission.

Inside the mayor's office the administrative assistant screamed when they splintered the door. Wearing a flowered dress, she toppled from her chair. The scoundrels seemed unconcerned about granting the poor woman even a crumb of decency; they left her untouched on the carpet with a fair amount of thigh exposed.

Hearing the commotion of pencils snapping and chairs being upset, the mayor emerged into the waiting room wearing a severe scowl. He figured it was unruly country boys bent out of shape about the new corn liquor tax.

The head scoundrel roared and made a gorilla gesture of fists-on-chest. Sweat spattered the air. "Glad you could make it, Mayor, to your own funeral and the funeral of your beloved town. This here is Lefty, Smelly, Blender, and Hobbs. And my name's Cunt."

The mayor's fear resigned to confusion. "Cut?"

"Cunt."

"Cud?"

"Cunt. You heard right. That ever-gaping wound upon the fairer sex."

The mayor maintained a neutral expression. He cleared his throat and said: "May I ask why you use that name?"

Cunt nodded to Smelly, who reached out and ripped off the mayor's blue collared shirt, leaving him in his cotton tank, which bore a yellowish stain. His hairy plump shoulders jiggled, and the scoundrels laughed.

"I gave myself the name to remember where I came from." Cunt's eyes were dead black holes. "From a mother who never wanted me, born into a world of hate." He grabbed a stapler from the desk and bit it in half. Plastic shards shot from his mouth as he spoke: "You might wonder why I didn't name myself something else. Something not so *vulgar*." He said the word in a high-pitched mocking voice, and the scoundrels giggled as if drunk or drugged.

"Maybe I should have named myself *womb*," Cunt snarled. "Wouldn't that be nice? Or the pretty *vagina*." The scoundrels snickered louder, but Cunt shushed them with an icy glare. "Tell me,

Mayor, if you could name yourself—any name in the world—what would it be?"

The mayor gave the question as much consideration as he could muster considering the circumstances. He knew two things: first, the local police force had as much force as a dryer sheet; these outlaws would puree Sheriff Holbrook and Deputy Barker when they arrived; therefore the weight of the moment hung on the mayor's shoulders, which currently were chilly and exposed. He'd never felt so helpless, except while watching his wife die.

"Well, Cunt, I appreciate your question." He assumed the smooth, confident politician voice honed during past election cycles. "In fact, the issue of naming is quite important to me. You see, my Christian name is Gale. Bestowed by my sweet mother, God rest her soul. A fine name, suggestive of powerful winds, the invisible forces guiding us all."

"Gale sounds like a woman," smirked Blender. Hot air puffed from his mouth and filled the mayor's nose with a bouquet of booze and rot.

"He got boobs like a woman," Lefty guffawed.

Cunt wasted not a moment in decapitating Lefty with the machete he had sheathed at his waist. The head fell to the carpet, followed by the twitching, spurting body.

"Anyone else disrupts my conversation and they will get raped by this here fist," Cunt warned, brandishing his hammer-like appendage.

Chided, the scoundrels looked at their boots.

"As I was saying, my given name is Gale." The mayor ventured a glance at the administrative assistant, who stirred behind the desk. He hoped she was OK and hoped equally that she wouldn't attempt any foolish heroics. "But as your colleague correctly noted—" the mayor glanced at Blender "—Gale is typically a woman's name."

A childlike look of pride overwhelmed Blender's oily face.

"You can bet that my schoolmates sought to disparage me with taunts and jabs not unlike those you yourselves have cast," the mayor said with a sad voice. "Naturally, I longed for a more masculine name."

"This guy's a word diarrhea factory!" yelled Smelly. "Let's move him already and get to running the town."

Wordlessly and barren of emotion, Cunt made good on his promise, disrobing Smelly with a strategic machete swipe and violating him with a clenched fist on the floor of the office. When he'd completed the vulgar act, he accommodated Smelly's pleadings to put him out of his misery by punching his head until he breathed no more.

Throughout the lengthy and horrific scene, the mayor remained motionless, as did Hobbs and Blender. Although not a religious man, the mayor took inventory in those moments, reflecting and considering on his actions in this lifetime. He had made mistakes, as any person did, even twice cheating on his dear wife. But that was long ago. He sincerely believed that he'd lived a moral existence, ready to step into the next world when such was his fate.

While the men endured the violation scene with statuesque stoicism, the administrative assistant Molly Reynolds stealthily positioned herself in a crouch behind the desk.

"Now," Cunt said to the mayor, "please continue."

The mayor had no idea why this monster, who could have snapped him in half with two fingers, was so interested in his opinion. Certainly scoundrels of these men's caliber had base designs on turning this beatific town—the town where the mayor was born and had lived his entire life, twenty years as a postal clerk before winning three consecutive mayoral terms—into an outpost of debauchery; of drug trafficking and prostitution, of greed and corruption, of gambling and bloodshed. A world where the only morality was power. Certainly their appetite for violence knew no limits. Certainly Cunt understood that once he, the mayor, was overthrown, there would be no one to impede his vigorous march toward domination.

Outside the window came a voice through a bullhorn: "Attention! This is the police." The mayor recognized Sheriff Holbrook's nervous, nasally timbre. "We have the building surrounded. Surrender your weapons peacefully and nobody gets hurt."

Cunt issued a barely perceptible nod, a twitch of the head, and Hobbs raced to the window and flung it open. Shouting Spanish obscenities, he pulled the ring from a grenade and tossed it onto the street. An explosion rocked the building, followed by silence and the charred stench of smoke. With a grim heart, the mayor understood that Holbrook and Barker had departed the earth.

"So I guess you still want your answer," the mayor said. He thought of his wife, who had passed away from cancer three years earlier. Only yesterday he'd placed flowers upon her grave and whispered that he loved her. He hoped that she had heard, but his rational mind told him he was merely speaking to the grass.

Cunt nodded with heavily lidded eyes, as if weary but determined to make it through this grueling exercise. The mayor continued. "So, after my rather disastrous stint in elementary school, I was only too ready to carve out a new identity in high school. Start fresh, you know. But in a small town like this, it's not really possible. Everybody knew me, so when I tried to get them to call me Skip, it just didn't catch on."

"Ahahaha, fucking *Skip*?" Hobbs hollered. "That's the stupidest name I ever heard!" His eyes suddenly widened in horror. "Dammit, Cunt, don't!"

But it was too late: Cunt snapped his neck. His corpse thudded onto Smelly's desecrated body.

"My personal difficulties lead me to think deeply on the subject," the mayor said. By now he understood that if he spun the story out for as long as possible, odds were good that the scoundrels would kill each other off. Only Cunt and Blender remained. "A name, I realized, is more than just a word attached to a person. A name is an identity. It is, in many ways, a reflection of our *self*, our personality—whether we like it or not, for good or for bad.

"So I waited, Cunt. I waited until my mother passed away. I realized that I couldn't erase the name she'd chosen; I couldn't kill off the self that my beautiful, kind-hearted mother had given me. And you know what? A funny thing happened. As the years went by, I began to see myself as my name. Like it or not, I was *Gale*. So I was determined to *be* Gale, at least while she was alive. To be that invisible force that moves people, that changes lives, that carries pollen from the flowers and seeds the soil in faraway fields."

Amazingly, tears had filled Cunt's eyes. His lips quivered.

The mayor wouldn't let himself be distracted. He had to finish his story. "By the time my mother passed away, I knew I would never change it. No more than I could decide to call the *sun* by a different name. So to answer your question, if I could choose any name it would be the one I was given: Gale Huggerbottom."

Like Cunt, Blender's eyes were also welling with tears, but the mayor could tell he was writhing painfully under the urge to laugh.

"I say it proudly to you now," the mayor said in a booming voice. "I am Gale Gaylord Huggerbottom."

Blender lost it, howling with laughter. And then he lost both arms, courtesy of Cunt's machete. Cunt kicked him bleeding out the window, and only one scoundrel remained.

Cunt was panting heavily from the work he'd done. "I'm glad you told me your story. And I'm glad you're accepting of who you are, because that is something I have never been." He groaned as if in pain, like a mother cat lowing for the death of her kitten. He raised the machete. But then he hesitated. A curl of a smile formed on his lips. His eyes glinted with recognition. He said, "Get out of here, Gale. Go live like the wind."

The mayor didn't move. He felt flooded with peace and resolve, a blissful emptiness inside him as if the wind of his name had cleared the debris from his soul. He spoke in a measured voice: "Well, then. Before I leave, I have one last thing to say. I respectfully disagree with you. It's a minor point, but an important one."

Cunt, the blood-spattered behemoth, gleaming and enraptured, awaited the mayor's wisdom.

"You say you haven't been able to accept who you are, but your name tells me otherwise." A mischievous smile crept across the mayor's face. "Because *cunt* is the filthiest word in our language. It's the word nobody wants, used only by the most ignorant losers, the true insects of society. It's a word that expresses nothing but idiocy and animal rage. It has as much poetry as a toenail. I daresay it lacks humanity. It's like a brick hurled into the ocean, swallowed by its own puerile insignificance." The mayor paused, catching his breath, knowing his fate. "And so for you, young man...Cunt is absolutely accurate. By taking that name and wearing it proudly as you do, you definitely accept what you are."

Cunt gripped the bloody machete, staring into space as if unsure how to proceed. Briefly, the mayor thought perhaps he could exit while Cunt was so engaged by whatever dull synapses were firing in his brain.

Before the mayor could take a step, Molly Reynolds rose behind her desk. She'd been a loyal, hardworking employee for three years. Always punctual. Polite and professional. From a Christian family. Highly attractive but garbed in a manner appropriate to the Office of the Mayor.

Now she wielded a shotgun, which was enormous against her petite shoulder. Her mascara was smeared, and her face was frenzied. "You don't talk about him that way," she said. She fired both barrels into Mayor Huggerbottom, killing him instantly.

She dropped the gun, maneuvered around the desk, and embraced Cunt, her sweaty musky Cunt. She licked droplets of carnage from his chest and grinned up at him.

"I couldn't stand him talking about you like that," she said.

Cunt considered, frowning. "All the same," he said, "perhaps they were words I needed to hear."

"No way. Trust me, he was a real ass."

"Still, he's got me reconsidering our plan. Am I capable of being the mayor of this town? Even with my awesome physical powers and extensive underworld connections, do I have it in me to be a leader of men? Or is it like Gale said? Have I destroyed my potential, my destiny, by naming myself in such a foul, classless fashion?"

Molly shrugged. She offered him a stick of spearmint gum because his breath smelled like death and whiskey. "A name is nothing but a name," she said. "Didn't Shakespeare say that?"

"I suppose so."

"Cunt for President. You got my vote."

He sighed wearily at the woman he loved. She was correct; a stink beetle was no less a survivor than a golden eagle. Destiny was a cold hard bitch; un-revisable. He'd labored hard in pursuit of this demolition, sacrificed four of his best horrible men to arrive at this moment, and the only recourse was to laugh like a splintered tree under the chainsaw assault.

So together, with blood-stained smiles, Cunt and Molly navigated the contortion of ruined bodies toward their brief, uncertain future.

Reborn

The priest wished the woman had opted to sit behind the screen. He recognized her as a regular at ten o'clock mass. She was a thick-bodied, seemingly simple girl—mid-20s and a newlywed, if he remembered correctly—with flat auburn hair that brushed her collarbones. Her floral dresses were modest and old-fashioned. Teamed with her freckles, the effect was of a Norman Rockwell painting.

"I have impure thoughts," she said. She looked at her wedding ring, studying it as if perceiving it for the first time.

"And these thoughts aren't of your husband," the priest said, filling in the blanks, trying to ease her anxiety.

She barked an ugly laugh that resembled a throat clearing. "I tell myself not to. But the more I resist, the more this man gets in my head."

The priest realized that the woman's outward innocence masked an indelicate, perhaps forceful, interior. Her eyes blinked rapidly as if trying to cool whatever fire burned inside her head. He wanted to help. "It's good for you to acknowledge these mental forays, but you've committed no deed. An impure idea isn't a moral reality."

With an unmistakable power that belied her words, she said: "This is difficult." She expulsed a hard breath and added, "The man is you."

Every encounter ended with the priest alone at the sink, praying for forgiveness.

He had walked through the Devil's Doorway with little provocation. He had been confident in his calling. Tempted on occasion, but never in danger. Once the boundary was crossed, however, his prior resistance meant nothing. With his failure he had nullified years of abstinence.

Mondays and Fridays, the woman parked her raspberry Saturn on the street, three blocks from the rectory.

★

He was the best the congregation had seen in forty years. He delivered sermons in a presidential cadence that filled the church without the aid of a microphone. From the most distant pew parishioners identified real joy in his smile. They left Mass feeling optimistic and strong, reassured by his parting handshakes and shoulder-squeezes.

Stately in his finery, diligent in his diet, an annual participant in the 15K Sprint for Splints, the priest was a picture. The women used this phrase—"He's a picture"—and their husbands did not disagree. "Lean and fit," they agreed. "Clean complexion." Although they would never admit it to their wives, the men envied the priest's hair, which commandeered his scalp like a battalion on Iwo Jima.

The priest knew that people responded to physical beauty; it was a scientific fact. The clipped Psychology Today article in his desk drawer pointed out that car salesmen with symmetrical faces sold 30% more than their nonsymmetrical coworkers.

In a very real way, nothing to be ashamed of, the Church was a commodity. He was selling Christ. You had to win people over, lure them from the distractions of the world.

He shaved twice a day, trimmed nose and ear hair, paid for a monthly salon cut, and gelled liberally. He received pedicures and manicures (for discretion he visited a suburban spa forty minutes away).

The priest would never tamper with God's vision—no plastic surgery, thank you. He didn't enjoy dwelling before a mirror. However, he would use every natural means to accentuate the positives in order created the best servant he could be.

★

She wasn't the greatest lover; in fact, their encounters were clumsy. The priest blamed himself and tried to speak to her about it, but she wouldn't. The topic of physical intimacy seemed distasteful to her. She wasn't standoffish, only complicated. Her silence signified to the priest that she held mysteries that he was eager to learn. She didn't speak badly of her husband, who was a heavy, red-faced pharmacist. She didn't condemn herself or the priest for their actions. She seemed only to want to be held and to appreciate the gentle tap of the ticking clock with him.

The priest couldn't pinpoint what was happening inside him. In the young woman's arms, he experienced a wave of connectedness to humankind. Her fingers, her bouquet, filled his senses. Out in the world, trivial sights appeared like miracles to his eyes—a leaf skating past on the pavement, a cloud stretching across the sky, a ripped sofa on a curbside. His lungs drew deeper breaths. He felt like he could dance across fire.

During one lovemaking session, possessed by this feeling of connection—which could only be described, he thought, as lust; a lust for life, lust for the very blood coursing through their human veins—the priest flipped the woman over and took her from behind. She gasped as if he had struck her, but then gradually began to rock in rhythm with his movement. Her throat chirped like a squeaky door, as if something inside her was in disrepair and this new action was revealing the damage for the first time. Her chirps changed to moans, almost mournful, burdened with hunger.

She pulled away and wrestled him onto his back. Straddling him, she brought herself to climax, grasping the priest's head roughly. She bucked and heaved. A handful of his hair tore free.

In the bathroom she positioned a mirror so he could view the damage. Her face was crumpled by an expression of despair so pronounced that the priest felt unsettled and frightened. He forced a lighthearted tone as he said, "No problem. It'll grow back."

Privately, he worried. He hadn't felt any pain when his hair came out. He'd felt nothing.

The next morning, while preparing for a meeting with the Diocese fathers, his comb ripped a nest from above his right ear.

The priest wondered if he was dying. Divine retribution weighed on his mind even though he knew that God didn't mete out punishment like a schoolmarm. The shedding, he told himself, could be attributed to stress (the stress of an affair that could jeopardize his career), but not to his savior.

★

Each morning, hair covered the priest's pillowcase. By the end of the summer, his head was bare except for sparse patching that resembled dead weeds. The young woman began crying during sex, but her cries weren't soft or gentle. Her tears seemed angry, and she made love with a grave fervor that unsettled the priest.

Aloud at Mass, he prayed—never for himself, but he made offerings on behalf of the parishioners who were desperate to save him. They donated thousands of dollars for his medical bills.

After months of tests, however, no cause or cure for the hair loss was found.

"I insist that you stop giving to me," he announced one day. "There are many in more desperate need than myself."

The crowd murmured, a wave of unrest. A woman shouted, "We'll never abandon you!"

"Your generosity touches me," he said. "But the doctors say there's no danger with my condition. It's purely cosmetic."

"We'll never abandon you!" another woman offered.

Their shouts took up the air.

Money flowed in at a record pace. New tests were administered with inconclusive results.

The priest learned that doctors used the word "inconclusive" instead of "I don't know." The word protected them.

In the privacy of his home, the priest stood in front of his mirror at every free moment. The hair loss wasn't only on his head. It was everywhere: chest, arms, legs, and groin were bare and smooth. Even his eyebrows disappeared.

The worse his appearance became, the more the priest gazed at himself. Undoubtedly, he'd been obsessed with his image for years—he felt mature enough now to admit this—but his deformity (as he thought of it) had seemingly made his narcissism worse. In naked detail he was able to see, with clarity, the core ugliness of his self. The skin atop his skull glowed a milky hue, marred by divots and gulleys. Some bald men looked attractive, but not him. I look like a planet, he thought.

Nights, he lay awake, caressing his smooth body. He was hideous, and he thanked God for it: He'd become a grotesque infant, but pure, stripped of sin and sexuality. He no longer felt desire for the young pharmacist's wife, or for any woman. God knew the importance of the priest's mission and had hit the rewind button. He was being given a second chance, and the priest would not squander it.

The woman did not take the news well.

"I'm not a fucking radio," she said. Her hair looked like an overzealous plant, curling in the humidity, wild, in stark contrast to the day she'd first come to his confessional. Ditches resided beneath her eyes. "You can't just turn me off when you're done with me." She hadn't been a Norman Rockwell painting for some time, but this attitude was something new.

The woman was having problems at home that the priest suspected were the source of her rage. Her husband was addicted to online gambling. The woman didn't know about his addiction, and the marriage was no doubt suffering under the strain of this secret. The priest had heard the fat pharmacist's confession but was prohibited by his vows from telling anyone. The priest studied the woman's shadowed face and worried about the potential scope of her retribution once he broke up with her.

Still, he had to do it. "This was wrong from the beginning," he said, trying to sound like he had all the answers. It was a tone he'd been perfecting since his ordination.

The woman studied her hand—a gesture he recognized from their first meeting—except this time she looked as if she were deciding what sort of weapon it could become.

"This was wrong from the beginning," he repeated.

She rolled away and faced the window. "Got it," she said. "I'm a mistake."

★

At the end of Sunday's mass, the young woman, wearing the floral Norman Rockwell dress, jogged to the podium.

The priest watched her with a sense of despair. Her lips were pursed in concentration. At the microphone she announced in a strong voice that she had something important to share. Would everyone please sit back down? She said she had a solution to the problem of the priest's condition. Their money was not solving the issue because the problem was not of worldly origin. It was a spiritual matter, and it required their devotion and their sacrifice. The parishioners, she implored, should donate hair instead of dollars. The crowd, momentarily stunned, lifted their hands and cheered.

Watching from the foyer, the priest felt the world falling away.

She passed him in the exit line. He said nothing, and neither did she. But while she shook his hand she slipped him a folded note.

★

Collection baskets were placed at the church entrance. Soon envelopes and bags stuffed with hair were piled high. The number of bald heads at mass multiplied, a fact the priest could not bring himself to publicly acknowledge. He didn't feel gratitude for their sacrifice. He felt rage. Hair was a privilege, not a right. Despite their good intent, these people were throwing away a God-given gift.

His father had been a barber: "Twenty heads a day for fifty-eight years" was his father's refrain during his final year of life. As a boy, the priest had spent summers in the shop, reading comics, flipping through baseball cards, fetching shaving lotion and pomade while his father made the scissors dance. A stroke killed his father, but those heads—400,000 strong—constituted an army.

★

It took eleven operations to sew the hair into the priest's skin. The surgeons began with his scalp, which quickly filled. Hair was then grafted to his chest, legs, and arms. A beard was built, and then a longer beard. The priest's shoulders were attended to, and the private regions.

The priest couldn't refuse a single donation. The young woman's note had made her terms unbearably clear.

Hair by the bushel rolled in, hair of every color and texture: soft, golden strands that smelled like sweet perfume; salt-and-pepper hair reeking of cigarettes; brittle gray curls; wispy infant down. Each strand found a home on the priest's body.

The young woman sat beside his hospital bed as he recovered. Her husband never accompanied her. They had gotten a divorce, although in the eyes of the Church they were still married.

"Why do the doctors get to say 'inconclusive'?" the priest asked. "I'm not allowed to use that word."

The woman continued knitting. Something red and drapey. She shrugged. "It doesn't matter now," she said. "Your point is moot."

"The question of why," said the priest, "is never moot."

The woman stood and pressed his morphine button a couple of times.

★

Fully recovered, the priest stood at the pulpit and faced his congregation. He was encased in a cocoon. From top to toe, the transplanted hair now lay eight inches thick. The world was muffled and distant, no longer visible to him. Would he ever gaze upon his own face again? Probably it was best if he didn't.

You have to lose yourself, the young woman had written, *the same way I lost myself in you.*

Reborn

He stood before his flock of shaven and shorn, expecting no answers and receiving none.

He raised his arms. Wings of hair brushed the floor. He knew it was affection and love that compelled his parishioners, so he didn't attempt to stop them. He allowed their furious applause to swell like a wave and crash over him. When the clapping died, rain could be heard whispering outside the windows.

The Lumping

By lumping, he said, we will become. Not by lumping on occasion, only when it is convenient, but with discipline and devotion, passionate at all times, with disregard for lesser obligations (clearly implying that every earthly obligation fell into this category). If everyone lumped three times a day, he stammered and sweated, ours would be a world of transcendence and joy. To lump is to live; to live, lump.

Naturally it would be difficult to make room in our lives for lumping. This he admitted as a wave of sadness passed over his face. Daily food shopping, arguments with husbands and wives, project reports due at the office, church gatherings, Tee ball games: such a plethora of distractions to be accounted for, to be superseded.

Here he removed a towel from his back pocket, dabbed his glistening brow, and thanked us for our courage in joining him on this fine evening when we had thousands of other non-lumping activities competing for our attentions.

Our culture, he said (and we were quietly thankful he included himself as a member) would love nothing more than to leave us all unlumped. The lump had gotten a bad rap. It was misunderstood, villainized, mocked in the media. Bad press all around. Was this a mere coincidence, or could there be—he hesitated before uttering the word—a conspiracy? Uneasy chuckles passed through the crowd, but his face remained stoic, suggesting that he found the possibility quite feasible.

He said our modern bodies longed to be lumped. The natural order demanded it, in fact, but time had made us forget. Thousands of years ago we had lumped without thought, with scarcely any conscious effort, with as much ease as we now slid on a pair of pants. Once upon a time life consisted solely of lumped people going about their business wearing blissful expressions of satisfaction. Our intrinsic need and ability to lump had been bred out of us, through no fault of our own, across the generations.

But the situation wasn't hopeless. His face lit with a mesmerizing smile, his eyes gleaming like polished stones. It would take diligence and dedication, he said, to retrain our primal instincts. We were soft, fragile beasts, spoiled and unchallenged by daily routine. Lumping, however, remained alive deep within us; what we needed was to simply tap into our recesses and let nature recapture the area where the daily grind had staked a bully's claim.

By lumping, he panted, stepping delicately along the length of the wooden stage as we tried to keep our eyes on him while furiously lumping (a difficult task), not only would our bodies sweeten and tone, but our hearts would follow suit. We would, in effect, lumpify our souls. With lumping, all of the desperation we felt, all of the disappointments in life—the failed promotions, the bad hair days, the parking citations, the unhappy marriages—these trivialities would cease to matter. Transcendence for all. A lump is invincible, he exclaimed, because a lump is legion.

A crowd had massed steadily around the stage. The wind no longer stirred. Our hot breath poured from our mouths. Had it only been hours since we'd arrived? It seemed much longer. We tried to recall our homes, our families, our obligations, but the memories were gone. Our attentions were set upon reaching this goal—his goal—the strange and tantalizing plateau of achievement that until this moment had not been conceivable.

A gauze of darkness pressed upon us as twilight fell. All around, people pushed for purchase, trying to get as near as they could in order to hear the lumping instructions. Throughout the crowd the lumping became more elaborate, more desperate, as our proficiency increased while we sensed an encroaching end. Was the stage equipped with lights? What would happen when nighttime was total? What if nobody achieved full lumpness?

The space was cramped, neighbors knocking elbows and treading toes. The air hung ripe with the bouquet of sweat. Everyone studied the man, seeking whatever key movement would complete the lumping process. But we all still looked the same, just like ourselves: pale, unfit, and frightened. Surely we had not lumped, were not even close. What were we doing wrong? Were we even capable of full lump? Did we lack the proper passion, the devotion?

On stage the man had been silent for some time, merely lumping to himself and observing the gathering disorder with a watchful gaze. At first glance he appeared tranquil, but in the waning light his face resembled the dark skin of a pond. Beneath its reposed surface swirled life, containing multitudes, bearing each one of us: our concerns, our failures, our secret regrets. He held our discontent within himself even as we tried to deny it.

Perhaps, we thought, this was the true meaning of lumping: to finally lay bare our most private selves, to unite through the world of the hidden, the inner place where heretofore none could live but the architects themselves. A playground where lumps could frolic: no names, no identities, no bodily trappings.

His lumped body finally came to rest. The cage of his chest swelled and shrank like the pulse of the world. Yes, he said. Now you understand.

The darkness grew quietly across our eyes as the cold chill of night swept into our bones, and together we raised our hand to the sky.

Session 4

Q: Describe what you see.

A: Once upon a time there was a man, a young adult. At the start of my story, let's say he's 24. This guy is bright, not stupid. Not brilliant, but above average. College graduate and all that. He is either fat or skinny; that part doesn't matter, so picture him however you would like. But probably a heterosexual white guy, because it's important that he never experienced anything in the way of discrimination or prejudice. Your basic middle-class Caucasian man growing up in America in the 21st century. I tend to picture him as a wiry dude who dresses in t-shirts of obscure rock bands and has lousy eyesight requiring thick glasses. But that's just me.

What's not up for debate is that he was generally a kind person, perhaps even to a fault. At least on the surface. However, *kind* might not be the most accurate descriptor. He was generally pleasant, but possessed a strong sensitivity to criticism and stress. So maybe instead of *kind* a better word is *weak* or *spineless*. At moments when others would stand up for themselves, he would shrink from conflict. For instance, one day he ordered a large vanilla latte with caramel sauce, but the barista gave him a caramel latte. He didn't even complain—he glanced around sheepishly as if wondering if anyone else had seen the error. Then he shrugged his shoulders and drank it! Was he a shrinking violet? Some kind of scaredy cat? He definitely wondered if he was, but I think you'd agree that most people question themselves in this way. You'd also be correct in asserting that the majority of people dislike conflict, dissonance, confrontation, rocking the boat. And this is exactly how the young man rationalized his behavior: *Hey, nobody enjoys fighting, so why should I?*

He lived in a brownstone apartment in Cincinnati. His employer was the Cincinnati History Museum. Deep in the museum basement he could be found in semi-darkness, his skin glowing bluish as he hunched in front of his computer. He was responsible for keeping meticulous records of the museum's holdings. It was a job he loved in large part because he worked in isolation: this guy did not like being around people. He wasn't shy, strictly speaking. Put him in a party scene and he did OK. He could talk about punk rock, the Bengals, Mediterranean cuisine. But when he conversed it was like he was mimicking the behavior of others. His gestures were stilted; his body language suggested anxiety; he was stiff and unrelaxed; he almost never asked people questions about themselves. Deep down, he just didn't *get* people. Which sounds weird, of course, since he himself was a person. It's similar to those adults who say, "I don't like kids." Um, you realize that *you* were a kid, right? Did you not like yourself then? Did you hate your friends when you were a kid? And by the way: at what point does a person stop being a kid? What's the magical line? Eighteen? Why eighteen? Why any age?

From his first-floor apartment in the brownstone he had a good view of the sidewalk. While at home this is where he preferred to sit, sipping coffee, watching people interact with each other. It fascinated him. What could they be talking about? For ten, fifteen, twenty minutes they would stand out there, chatting with total strangers. *I've got a dog. You've got a dog. Let's talk about my dog, and then let's talk about your dog. Dogs are great.* God, what the hell? Strangers just blathering on: how did they do it? How could they waste their time like that? It gave him a headache it was so confusing. Part of him wished he could hear what they were saying, but another part of him suspected whatever it was would be so lame, so trivial, and so *purposeless* that he would lose faith in all of humanity.

Deep down, this guy was motivated by a deep insecurity. Essentially he was unconvinced about his worth to society. Naturally, as any good Freudian will tell you, he was not consciously able to confront this insecurity. His psychic defense had to construct a system that would allow him to live with a modicum of internal balance, and therefore his insecurities were repressed and replaced by an out-of-control ego. In other words, he believed himself to be superior to everyone. In order to feel deserving of the life he'd been given—which, let's be honest, is chock full of ridiculously unfair advantages for a middle-class white boy—he needed to believe that others' lives were vapid, superficial, unchallenging, and on and on.

As you can imagine, such an attitude wears a person down. Sunrise, sunset. Years rolled by. Before he knew what hit him he had reached middle-age. Not surprisingly, he remained unmarried. Women who were his intellectual equal or superior—on the surface, women who should stimulate and challenge him in the best of ways—were summarily broken up with or avoided altogether. The simpler women, less educated, absent of hobbies, un-opinionated, or otherwise perceived by him to be uninteresting, were also dropped. Over time the man adopted a predictable pattern of entering a relationship, professing intense feelings for the woman in question, and then abruptly sabotaging the relationship: picking fights over trivial issues; finding fault with everything she did, whatever.

By the time he celebrated his 50th birthday (a quiet affair attended by his brother, mother, father, and sole friend from college), the man was mostly bald. His waist was eight sizes larger than when he was in his 20s. He still worked at the museum, although he had grudgingly accepted a promotion to supervisor. Now he was tasked with making work schedules, keeping computers operational, and managing a modest crew of young men and women who were doing the same job he'd done when he started.

Session 4

Whenever he stepped out of the shower and looked at himself in the mirror, he was repulsed by what he saw. Once a slender, not-bad-looking man with nice lips and thick hair, he was now a flabby, fat dude with gross patches of hair all over his pale body (except his head, where the remaining hair was like a sad puff of tumbleweed). He didn't even recognize the old man in the mirror and avoided his own reflection whenever possible.

He reminded himself that physical appearance wasn't important; this had never mattered to him; he'd always mocked the people who were insecure about their looks. So superficial! What was *inside* was the important thing! Truthfully, he'd been fortunate for most of his life. He had good genes that meant he never had to worry about obesity or acne or any of the other trappings of insecurity.

Now he had to admit it: he understood where people were coming from. When your body isn't what you think it should be, it's like you're living inside another person. You walk to the store, eat your dinner, watch television, etc. You know that you are "you," but there's a feeling of disconnect, as if you're merely a consciousness residing inside a borrowed body. You observe as things happen to the body, but from a distance, like you're the commander of a big robot. You're able to control the robot and feel what the robot feels on the surface—the pain of a stubbed toe; the glare of bright sunlight—but on a very real level you understand that none of this is affecting *you*.

So the man got older. His skin hardened, wrinkled, crinkled, and flaked. Vision got worse. Bowels became less cooperative. His parents flew the coop, bought the farm, all of that. His friend moved across the country and lost touch.

He retired with a good package, was financially all set. If he had desired, he now had the time and money to travel to all the places he'd once imagined: Rome, Amsterdam, Barcelona.

Instead, he whiled away the days surfing the Internet and renting movies. He fed the body, scrubbed its aging flesh, visited the doctor for chest pains, and never quite allowed his brain to acknowledge what he had become. At long last, he had transformed into the very thing he had always hated: a stranger. Remember, he considered himself superior to other people; and now he had become one of them. Yes, he couldn't stand being around himself! He couldn't come up with anything to say—or even to think—because he knew that *he himself was uninteresting*. He wasn't even interested in small talk with his own brain.

All of this sounds pretty depressing. But in another way, you could argue that this guy had achieved a higher plane of existence. He had moved beyond the corporeal. Transcended the base needs and desires of the Self. Unchained himself from the physical world and its attendant hungers. Stepping outside the ego and letting go of base needs are the ultimate goals of every religion, from Buddhism to Christianity to Islam. Almost in spite of himself, without even trying, he had achieved Oneness with the universe.

Or maybe he was just an asshole.

Or maybe he was both, simultaneously: an asshole and a god.

Or maybe it's *necessary* to be both. Maybe reaching Nirvana on earth means being a socially awkward, introverted, selfish, lonely, disconnected, superior, inferior, judgmental, unmotivated, insecure, cocky, un-athletic human blob.

Q: I'm sorry, I tuned out a while back. What were we talking about?

Acknowledgements

Jerry Brennan for his tireless efforts, keen eye, and steady, supportive disposition. Robert Fanning, Jeffrey Bean, and Matt Roberson for being the finest colleagues. C.G. Simons for reminding me that it does not look like a baton. Simon and Charlie for the unrelenting nonsense. The graduate students of ENG 694: Craft of Fiction (Spring 2015), whose brave explorations and boundary-pushing directly inspired much of this collection. And librarians everywhere, especially my personal librarian Courtney, for being pushers to each new generation.

Gratefully acknowledged are the magazines in which these stories first appeared:

"Blackout" in *Main Street Rag Anthology: Commutability*;

"If the Invisible Man Dies and Nobody Sees it, Does He Really Die?" in *Redivider*;

"Engagement" in *Newfound Journal*;

"A Four-Letter Word for Exchange" in *Pure Coincidence*;

"Sanguine" in *Hobart*;

"Waterfowl" in *Spelk*;

"A Fine Time" in *(b)OINK*;

"D.T. Myse's *Cold Blood from a Scorched Cat: Sweet Whiskers in the Grip of Death*" in *Cockroach Conservatory*;

"Session 1" in *Five:2:One #thesideshow*;

"Party Town" and "Three Men on a Boat" in *The Pleasure You Suffer: A Saudade Anthology*, Tortoise Books;

"Insert Name" in *Summerset Review*;

"Twilford Baines, Buck Hunter Unbounded" in *Route 7 Review*;

"Snow, Lightly Falling" in *Squawk Back*;

"The Lumping" in *Passages North*;

"The Search for Boyle" in *Word Riot*;

"The Kids in West End" in *The Offbeat*;

"Festivity" in *Moonchild Magazine*;

"Outline" in *Okay Donkey*;

"Session 1," "Session 2," "Session 3," and "Session 4" in *Five:2:One Print Edition*

About the Author

Darrin Doyle has lived in Saginaw, Kalamazoo, Grand Rapids, Cincinnati, Louisville, Osaka (Japan), and Manhattan (Kansas). He has worked as a paperboy, mover, janitor, telemarketer, pizza delivery driver, door-to-door salesman, copy consultant, porn store clerk, freelance writer, and technical writer, among other jobs. After graduating from Western Michigan University with an MFA in fiction, he taught English in Japan for a year. He then realized he wanted to pursue fiction writing and permanently stop doing jobs he didn't love, so he earned his PhD from the University of Cincinnati.

He is the author of the novels Revenge of the Teacher's Pet: A Love Story (LSU Press) and The Girl Who Ate Kalamazoo (St. Martin's), and the short story collection *The Dark Will End the Dark* (Tortoise Books). His short stories have appeared in *Alaska Quarterly Review*, *Blackbird*, *Harpur Palate*, *Redivider*, *BULL*, and *Puerto del Sol*, among others.

Currently he teaches at Central Michigan University and lives in Mount Pleasant, Michigan with his wife and two sons. His website is www.darrindoyle.com.

About Tortoise Books

Slow and steady wins in the end—even in publishing. Tortoise Books is dedicated to finding and promoting quality authors who haven't yet found a niche in the marketplace—writers producing memorable work that will stand the test of time.

www.ingramcontent.com/pod-product-compliance
Lightning Source LLC
LaVergne TN
LVHW040614250326
834688LV00035B/546